W9-DFA-800

Insanity, Inc.

CAROLYN MCKINNON, RN

Illustrations by Charles J. Cronin

AUDENREED PRESS

Copyright © 1996 by Carolyn McKinnon, RN

All rights reserved, including the right of
reproduction in whole or in part in any form.

Places, events and characters are imaginary.
Any resemblance to persons living or
dead is purely coincidental.

Library of Congress Card Catalog Number 95-78037

International Standard Book Number 1-879418-97-5

Manufactured in the United States of America

AUDENREED PRESS

A Division of Biddle Publishing Company
P.O. Box 1305
Brunswick, Maine 04011
207-833-5016

Cover design by Charles J. Cronin

To Jim and our children,
  Mike, wife Mary Liz and children Katie, Chris and Meghan
  Ron, wife Barb and children Heidi, Melissa, Chris and Logan
  Shaun, wife Cheryll and son Michael
  Jeannine, husband Mark and children Jamie and Jacob
  Bill and wife Debbie
  John
to my special niece
  Laurie, husband Kyle and children Maddy and Katelyn
to our families and friends,
and to the memory of our loved ones who have gone before us

To my *other* families,
  the past and present members of the St. John's Catholic Church Choir, Bangor, Maine, and the Bangor Community Chorus who have given a special meaning to my life for many years

To the loyal, efficient teachers of A SMALL WORLD Day-Care Center

And to all those confined to mental institutions

ACKNOWLEDGMENTS

I would like to thank the following people for their help and support during the writing of this book: my husband Jim for his patience and behind-the-scenes support; my son John for his invaluable assistance; the nurses and other care-givers, without whose contributions this book would not have been possible; editor Julie Zimmerman for keeping me on track; Charles J. Cronin for his remarkable cover and illustrations; and my family and friends for their encouragement, especially Delphine O'Brien and Claudette O'Connell.

ILLUSTRATIONS

TABLE OF CONTENTS

PART I

DEATH OF THE ROYAL GUARD

CHAPTER ONE

Laurie Canaday felt serenely happy as she drove up the winding, tree-lined road to keep her appointment with the Nursing Director at Dunton State Mental Institution. It was good to be home again in Somerset, and she knew she was making the right decision. She had grown up in the busy town below, gone away to junior college and nursing school, and had then spent three years working at Boston General, a large, impersonal hospital with a constant turnover of patients. She was ready to work in an institution with long-term patients where she would feel more like a member of the family than a distant relative.

"It's so removed from the world up here, the way I always imagined it would be," she thought, leaving her car in a small parking area and taking in the view from the Hill. It reminded her of what it would be like to live as a nun in a sanctuary, living a peaceful life and serving God by caring for the poor souls inside. Most of them had been brought here against their wills, and most of them would die here. But that was where her job came in, to make the patients more comfortable, and maybe even give some meaning to their lives, some purpose, some reason for wanting to live.

She climbed the high flight of stairs, and entered the massive brick structure. Turning to close the big door behind her, she caught a glimpse of several patients busy at work in a beautiful rock garden on a small incline on the other side of the parking lot.

"Yes, I could be very happy working here," she thought, walking down the corridor to the switchboard to announce her arrival. In a moment, a middle-aged nurse with a kindly smile came to greet her and ushered her to the Nursing Director's office which was located on the 'male side' of the Main Building.

"You'll have a lot to get used to, Miss Canaday," Nurse Maybury said, standing up to shake hands with her new recruit. Grace Maybury cleared her throat dramatically and gave Laurie a long, cold look, sizing her up and getting right down to the business at hand.

"You'll have a lot of rules to learn," she said, sitting down and motioning for Laurie to do the same. "But you'll get used to them. Some of them I made myself, but Dr. Atherton, our Superintendent, is the real power *behind* the throne."

She laughed quickly, then was completely serious again. "No, I shouldn't have said he's the power behind the throne, since he's still very obviously in charge. It's just that he's been gettin' a little tired lately. He works so hard. Too hard, but I wouldn't dream of advisin' him to slow down, since he'd only ignore me."

She hesitated for a moment, then sighed and went on. "I've been workin' at Dunton for more years now than I care to mention. Dr. Atherton himself chose me to become his Nursing Director when the position became available about ten years ago, and we've been workin' together happily ever since. We share the same philosophy, I might say, regardin' how to rule the staff and care for the patients. You'll learn a great deal more about Dr. Atherton soon enough, and of course, if you decide to work here, I'll introduce you to him as soon as your application has been approved.

"But where was I? Oh yes. I had to work my way up to Nursing Director, and that took some doing, let me tell you. My first assignment was charge nurse of the female infirmary ward housing patients with chronic disabling conditions. It's no secret that I rule with an iron fist, not just nursing, but the clerical, housekeeping, recreational, kitchen, and laundry personnel. If you are to work up here, I warn you that you must do only as you are told, and keep your nose out of places where it does not belong. Is that clear?"

Laurie swallowed hard and said, "Yes, Ma'am."

Later that night, as she lay in bed in her old room, too nervous and excited to sleep, Laurie went over her first impressions of the staff and patients at Dunton, and although she had met a large group of people, she remembered Grace Maybury best of all. A large-boned, buxom woman, she had thick dyed red hair, and steel blue eyes that cut like a knife into Laurie's very thoughts.

An episode flashed in front of her eyes. She hadn't had the time to think much about it when it happened, but she recalled hearing Maybury shout at a young female aide, her high-pitched voice getting higher and louder and shattering the air like an ice pick, hammering away at the poor girl's nerves. "She hardly asked me about myself," Laurie thought. "She just talked on and on about her own power as if it didn't really matter who I was, as long as I listened to her."

Laurie felt a shiver go down the back of her neck as she contemplated those places where her nose would not belong, and the secrets they could tell.

It might have been wiser for her to say, "No, I don't think it'll work out for me up there on the Hill."

But Laurie Canaday wasn't a person to give up easily, especially when her mind was made up. No, this young woman was almost as stubborn as her superiors would prove to be, and it would be an uphill battle for her, working at Dunton, but a battle worth fighting, since it would be the battle of her life!

Laurie got up and pulled aside the curtains at her window to get a breath of whatever breezes might be blowing outside. She had grown up in this attic room in her parents' house, and her mother had kept things pretty much as Laurie had left them, almost eight years ago.

Eight years ago, when she was seventeen, there was a boy in her graduating class who might have been...who might have been her lover, if only she hadn't gone away to school. Perley Graves was a tall, blond young man who had been interested in many things -- basketball, football, science and anything mechanical in nature, and anything that had to do with Laurie.

"He had a crush on me, that was all," she thought, sitting with her legs crossed and her back against the window frame.

"Oh, I'm too old to be thinking about Perley now, and sitting here this way, the way I used to all through high school on those long, hot summer nights."

She had worked at summer jobs throughout her high school years, painfully saving as much of her salary as she could spare, so that one day she could go to nursing school. She'd always wanted to be a nurse, ever since her childhood, when she had "fixed" the broken arms and legs of her dolls and stuffed animals, bandaging them loosely with strips of torn sheets, then unraveling the mess and starting all over again until she got it just right, that is, tight enough for the bandages to stay on for a day or two without cutting off the blood supply of her victims...or rather, her "patients."

Her parents were middle class and well-educated, but her mother had come from the generation of women who didn't get jobs of any kind, simply because it would have been an embarrassment to their husbands. So even though Mrs. Canaday had a great deal of spare time on her hands, she had never gone to work, and had tried, unsuccessfully, to talk her daughter out of choosing a career, especially in such a demanding profession.

"They'll work you from sunrise to sunset," she had said, trying to counsel Laurie and convince her that she was making a mistake. "And it'll just break your heart, dear, to see so much sickness and death. Oh dear, I've never even seen a dead body, and I just don't know how you can stand it."

But Laurie had laughed away her mother's fears and tales of woe. "Gee, Mom, you're just not keeping up with the times. Women do all kinds of things today, and some of my friends have even asked me why I won't study to become a doctor! But it's always been my dream to be a..."

"I know, dear," her mother had said, "to be a nurse. But won't you find it distasteful, emptying bed pans and changing sheets? Giving sick people baths and walking them to the bathroom? It's always sounded so depressing to me. Couldn't you work with healthy people instead?"

"But healthy people wouldn't need my help, Mother! And besides, remember when I saved Mousetrap's life? I made up my mind, then and there, that I'd become a nurse one day, and that's just what I'm going to do!"

Mousetrap was Laurie's cat who had almost died one day after Joey Smith, the neighborhood bully, had thrown a rock at her, crushing her leg. But Laurie had nursed her back to health, cursing Joey Smith's name under her breath and vowing to beat him up some day. She had even tried convincing her boyfriend, Perley, to sneak up on Joey in a dark alley somewhere and teach him a thing or two. But Perley was far too shy, and probably fifty pounds too light, to beat up anyone, especially anyone as meanly aggressive as Joey Smith.

Yes, Perley was shy. Laurie wasn't even sure why she had loved him -- maybe for that very reason, she knew that he would never hurt her. Being the kind of boy who seemed to fade into a classroom so that you hardly noticed if he was there or not, Perley was perhaps the most obvious choice for her affections, since he seemed to need so much. At seventeen, Laurie believed that she could be everything Perley would ever need in a woman. Yes, she could be everything to Perley, if only he would show her that he cared.

But part of the problem came from the fact that Perley was too timid to show his love. He never did beat up Joey Smith, of course. And when the chance came for him to ask her not to go away after high school, Perley let it go by, letting her slip out of his life forever...or so he thought. He had been convinced that Laurie would become a nurse anyway, whether she married him or not, so he had to let her go away to school.

He couldn't have stopped her, in any case, but he didn't know then that she would develop an almost single-minded interest in her pursuit of a career. And Perley never knew that as the years passed, her love for him would wither and fade away into merely a memory, into a pleasant but distant nostalgia for the past.

Yes, it was pleasant to think of him again, to wonder what had become of him. But he was just a ghost to Laurie now, and there simply wasn't any time left in her life for a ghost.

After making up her mind to accept the job at Dunton, Laurie was formally hired as the three-to-eleven shift supervisor in the building they called the Atherton Annex. As its Chief Supervisor and Grace Maybury's right-hand woman, Lula Bagley, RN summarized it, the Annex was the newer of the two buildings comprising the Institution. The other was the massive, brick, century-old structure known as the Main Building. Housing the more infirm patients, the horseshoe-shaped Annex was divided into two sides. Those patients who were able to take care of their personal needs with minimal assistance were placed on the 'up side', where they were expected to do simple chores. It was the rare case that improved enough to be sent back into the world. Undesirable behavior was controlled by drugs.

Patients who were physically disabled and bedridden were placed on the 'bed side' in neat rows, cared for in routine, assembly-line fashion as though not living. Laurie found out in the first few days of her training, that Main-Building aides who weren't respectful enough to their superiors were transferred to the Annex until they either shaped up or were shipped out.

Included as part of Laurie's orientation was a complete tour of the Main Building, guided by Supervisor Lula Bagley. As they entered its huge door, Laurie wished that they could have used the word sanctuary, refuge, or retreat instead of the horrible sounding "mental institution", with all of its sinister connotations.

As the steel door to a 'back ward' on the 'male side' clanged shut behind them, Laurie's eyes were drawn to the floor, totally unprepared for the tragedy that began to play itself out in front of her. White-clad forms lined either side

of the long, barren corridor. Some of these human forms were curled up in fetal positions as though trying to regress to a stage when life was more merciful. Others sat apathetically on heavy wooden benches, staring blankly into empty spaces in front of them, or walked about aimlessly, pacing the same rhythmic, dead-end patterns on the floor like zoo animals in cages.

As they proceeded down the ward with its curtainless, barred windows, Nurse Bagley explained, "This is a total-care ward. The patients on this ward are almost totally dependent for their personal needs. Some of them will feed themselves though, if you set up their trays and give them a little assistance."

Laurie caught a glimpse of an attendant mopping an adjoining room, one of the several sleeping units ranging from two to twelve-bed size.

"We maintain high standards of cleanliness here," Bagley continued, apparently looking straight through the patients as if they were inanimate, lifeless props on a stage, and concentrating on the condition of the ward itself, as if the clean floors and bedsheets were more important than the patients who walked on them and slept in them.

"These floors are all dry and wet-mopped at least once every shift, and of course as necessary in between for puddles and 'deffie'."

"These patients aren't continent?" Laurie asked, walking quickly to keep up with her guide.

"Most of them aren't. That's why they're dressed in johnnies and slippers."

"What about the ones who are? Couldn't they be dressed?"

Nurse Bagley gave Laurie the kind of look that said, "Don't you know anything?" But she said, "It would be too much trouble keeping all that clothing straight. It's much easier just having them all alike. Every patient is checked three times every shift, and washed and changed if necessary. They also receive a bath once a week, and the ones who are especially messy get two. We maintain high standards of care here!"

As they approached the next heavily-barred and locked door, Nurse Bagley said, "Most of the patients on this ward are 'good' patients."

"What do you mean?" Laurie said.

"The 'good' ones just lie around or sit quiet and don't make any trouble. They don't even seem to respond when we talk to them, or give them their baths or medication. We don't have the staff here to give much psychotherapy, but we're proud of the care we provide. Undertakers tell us that the bodies from this Institution are in better condition than the bodies they get from any hospital around."

CHAPTER TWO

When Nurse Bagley opened the door to the female violent ward, a throng of patients dressed in sacks with holes cut for their heads and arms, stampeded towards her. Laurie wanted to run for safety, but there was nowhere to run. Hands grabbed at her arms, legs and neck, and a young teenage girl stretched out her arms in a desperate, unsuccessful attempt to hug her.

"They don't see a new face around here too often," Supervisor Bagley said, as a young, drooling, retarded woman planted a wet kiss on Laurie's cheek.

Feeling fingers pinching the calves of her legs and snaking their way up her body to the back of her neck, Laurie turned to see a tiny woman with devilish eyes looking up at her.

"You know what I've got?" the woman said, "I've got a pocket in my throat where I keep pins and needles." Then she coughed and exposed pin-heads and the tips of needle shafts sticking out of her mouth. "My family wanted to put me in the circus, because of my great abilities, but they put me in here instead." She swallowed hard, and the pins and needles disappeared.

"Isn't it terribly dangerous for her to have those...?" Laurie began, but Bagley didn't seem to hear her, or preferred to look the other way and not admit that anything was out of the ordinary. Nothing was ever out of the ordinary on the violent wards.

"All right, ladies," Bagley said, in a voice that reminded Laurie of a strict schoolmaster or riot-policeman, "Get back in your places."

Laurie hadn't imagined that these patients could have their own places, as Bagley had intimated, but at the sound of her stern voice, they retreated, some of them walking backwards and never taking their eyes off the two nurses. And it seemed as if each patient had her own territory, very carefully but invisibly marked out, since even mental patients needed to believe that they had some privacy, some measure of dignity.

Laurie shook her head sadly.

"We'd better be getting back to Maybury's office," Bagley said, interrupting Laurie's train of thought as she re-opened the steel door, letting Laurie pass through it and then locking it on the other side. Laurie breathed a sigh of relief, as if she'd just awakened from a horrible nightmare. But it didn't bring her the relief of knowing that her dream had been "unreal". In this case, waking and dreaming existed on the same level of reality, and so the nightmare would just keep on being there, behind the locked door, through day and night, awake or sleeping.

Nurse Maybury made the exception of breaking her routine by having lunch with Laurie and another young nurse named Sharon Lovejoy.

"I've asked Lovejoy to join us," Maybury was saying as they stood in the lunch line, moving their trays slowly along the counter. She works on the male admission ward, and I thought you could work with her this afternoon to get yourself accustomed to our procedures."

Sharon Lovejoy gave Laurie a sympathetic smile, and Laurie liked the young woman right away. She and Laurie looked somewhat alike. Both were slim, about five feet four, with dark brown hair. Laurie was struck immediately by the resemblance, and wondered if they would have similar ideas and tastes, as well as looks. She would need a good friend, working in this place.

Although Laurie hoped to make friends with as many of her co-workers as possible, she was still somewhat shaken by her morning experience. It was hard for her to suddenly turn off her depressing thoughts and act happy, as she would have liked to do on her first day at work, to give her superiors the impression that she was cheerful and helpful. But she didn't think she could say very much right now, and took only a soft roll and a glass of milk for lunch.

Sharon Lovejoy nodded at Laurie's tray with an understanding look. She had come to Dunton two years ago after graduating from nursing school with dreams of helping to treat people and not simply to keep their bodies clean. Now, she had come to a kind of resignation, as if she'd already given up her dream, since it seemed so incurably adolescent, compared with the reality of working at Dunton.

Yes, it had been a silly, childish dream, and by now she had almost forgotten her disappointment in herself for having failed to reach her goals, and for having cherished such unrealistic goals to begin with.

"We don't coddle our aides," Grace Maybury said, turning to Laurie and looking her straight in the eye as she spoke. Let me tell you about the way we work. RNs get every other weekend off, but the aides work a forty-eight hour week and have every sixth weekend off. They gripe about having to work six days in a row for six weeks, but how else do they expect to get Saturday and Sunday off together?"

"Anyway, don't let them see you sympathizin' with them. We have enough trouble with them already without someone addin' fuel to the fire. Since you're new, they'll be tryna feel you out to see if you're on their side or not. They'll try to convince you of how hard they have to work, but if you're wise, you won't let them get by with anything. Let me warn you, they'll play one supervisor against the other."

A voice came over the paging system, calling for Miss Lovejoy to report to the admissions office. Laurie accompanied Sharon so that she might observe the procedure. So the two younger women said good-bye to Grace Maybury, cleared off their trays and wound their way through the maze-like hallways leading back to the front of the Main Building.

When they walked into the admissions office, Laurie felt her jaw drop. She let out a tiny gasp of recognition as she saw that the man being admitted was her old dear boyfriend, Perley Graves.

She might not even have recognized him, if they'd been passing each other on a crowded downtown street. He was unmistakably identifiable as a deeply troubled man. He seemed shorter to her, or maybe that impression was caused by the way his shoulders and head sagged down. His hair was already flecked with gray, and his eyes and skin had the dull pallor of a man who'd been indoors for a long time, out of the sunlight and fresh air.

"Definitely depressed," someone muttered, and Laurie wasn't sure where the voice had come from, since Perley's brother and his wife were standing behind him, and there were two or three other hospital employees in the room. A doctor was sitting at the desk and helping Perley's brother to fill out the admission forms.

As Perley paced the floor, wringing his hands and trying to keep from crying, his brother said, "All he wants to do is lie down on his bed. He hasn't worked in months, since he can't concentrate on anything. Oh, he's been this way before, but never this bad."

Perley kept his eyes glued to the floor, and Laurie didn't know whether he would have recognized her or not. The doctor nodded and said that the committal papers seemed to be in order. Then Sharon leaned over and whispered into Laurie's ear, "This isn't a voluntary admission, you understand. If it were, the patient would be signing the papers himself. So watch out, there may be some trouble. If he resists, they may have to take him by force and restrain him."

There wasn't any trouble, though, since Perley seemed too distraught to struggle against his own fate. The doctor then handed the admission orders to the aide, who handed them over to Laurie to look through. The orders read, "Regular diet. Restrain prn for patient's own protection. Mellaril 25 mgm. three times daily. Thorazine 50 mgm. as necessary for agitation. Dalmane 30 mgm. for sleeplessness."

Laurie looked up from the orders just in time to see Perley's brother reach out his hand, but Perley wouldn't take it, and averted his face. As his brother and sister-in-law walked away, a single small muscle in Perley's cheek started twitching, giving him a feeble, pathetic appearance, as if he were a little boy being put into an orphanage, or worse, into a prison that would lock him away forever.

Sharon and Laurie followed as Perley was led into the Supervisor's office by an aide and attendant from the male admission ward. Here, his pockets were emptied, and his watch and ring removed. And it reminded Laurie of booking a man into jail when his money was counted, jotted down on a list, and placed in an envelope to be sent to the Steward's Office.

The aide was already acting as if Perley could do nothing for himself, and it seemed so presumptuous of her to reach intimately into his pockets and take out his things, as if even his own belongings -- his last reminders of the outside world -- were being taken from him. Couldn't she have asked him to do it himself? Or didn't she think that he was capable of performing even the most simple, everyday ritual of taking off his own watch?

Laurie almost stepped up to her old friend to say hello and tell him everything would be all right, but she didn't want to cause him any further embarrassment than he was already suffering, so she thought she would wait to talk to him later, after a day or two when he'd be adjusted to his new surroundings...and when she too would feel more at home here, if such a thing were possible.

Then the time came for Perley to be led to the ward. He started crying, saying that he didn't want to be admitted. Laurie watched helplessly as he was pulled and tugged by the aide and attendant, both trying to console him as best they could, saying that he needed to come to Dunton until he felt better again. At the locked door, he gave one last tug, but he might have been a child, tugging on two oxen, for all the good it did.

He was taken to the Tub Room, just inside the admission ward, where it was explained that he must now have a bath and shampoo. "We'll be sending your clothes up to the Marking Room," the aide said, "after we undress you and check you for any bruises or identifying marks."

And when she started to describe the delousing process that he would be undergoing, Perley sighed so deeply and sadly that Laurie's heart went out to him.

Then he looked up, his eyes met hers, and she noticed a flicker of recognition. But it passed in an instant, and maybe he had just recognized her as another human being, as a nurse who might help him out of this impossible, insane situation.

"Please help me," he said. That was all, just those three little words. He would say them to her many times again, without ever realizing who it was standing by him throughout his long agony and dying.

CHAPTER THREE

Driving down the long winding road back into the town of Somerset, after her third day of working at Dunton, Laurie was troubled.

"I feel as if I've been working there all my life," she thought, rounding a curve and pulling up to a stop light at a busy intersection.

When the light turned green, she accelerated again, and suddenly realized what was bothering her.

"They're like the rulers of a small kingdom," she thought, checking her rear-view mirror unconsciously, "with complete control over the Institution...everyone included. And who held the reins of power? Dr. William Atherton had been ruling the Institution for twenty-five years. His authority was absolute and unchallenged. Laurie had met him only briefly. He was a short, balding man who always had a cigar in his mouth. Since he was a strict disciplinarian, his people toed the mark for him. But they respected and almost revered him as a stern father figure. He didn't have much finesse, and as Lula Bagley put it, "He doesn't pull any punches."

He was often accused of taking a patient's word over that of an aide. "Aides can be picked up off the street any time," he often said, "for a dime a dozen, so I'd better not find any evidence of mistreatment of these patients, or out you go."

While Laurie would never get to know him personally, she and everyone else connected with Dunton were affected by his authority. He seemed more like an invisible presence, his name being whispered throughout the halls and wards like a magic incantation.

"He's certainly not democratic in any way," Laurie thought, pulling up to her parents' house and parking her car, "but he runs Dunton very efficiently. Everyone seems to know exactly what his duties are and performs them without question."

But she was still disturbed by something unspoken in the back of her mind. Something definitely made her uneasy, that she couldn't shake off. "But what is it," she thought, "and why can't I give up the idea that...something is terribly wrong?"

A vision of Mathilda Hoxie, Aide Supervisor Assistant, appeared before Laurie as she was running a bath for herself and planning to soak in it for a long time, to ease the tension out of her body and to "get away from it all," for a while. Mathilda was a tall, lanky woman with long, shapeless legs. She was fair complexioned, with baby-fine frosted hair that hung well below her shoulders. Her face on the whole was attractive, although her features, taken individually -- small blue eyes, thin lips and a long pointed nose -- gave Laurie the impression of a...?"

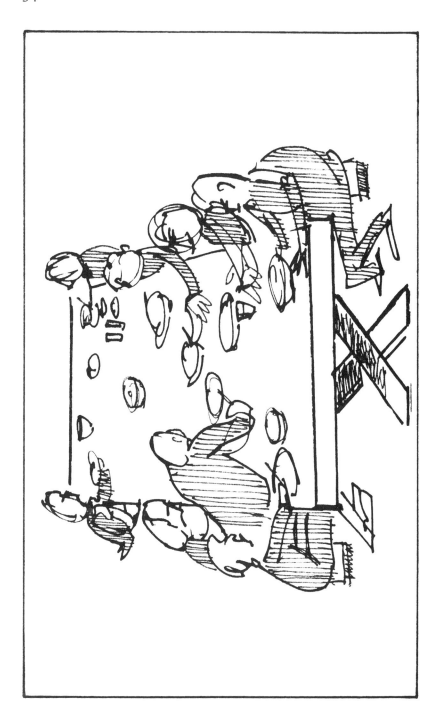

Snitch was the word that flitted through Laurie's mind, but she had no reason to make such a judgment, and was only going on the hearsay of two aides she'd just met. "I can't let myself believe in any gossip yet," she thought, lowering herself into the water, leaning her head back on the rim of the tub, and closing her eyes.

But Mathilda's face appeared before her, and she lived through the afternoon's experience all over again, as if it were just happening.

Mathilda, as a supervisor assistant, had access to all the wards, and was giving Laurie a complete tour of the Annex, showing her how to find the basement laundry room, drug room, and sterilizing room. They stopped to inspect the new, well-equipped modern kitchen, where she talked with one of the dietary staff about ordering more bananas.

Then a male dietary technician spoke up. "The aides have been complaining that my boys have been pickin' up the food carts too early and they've had to rush through feedin' the patients. But my boys tell me that your aides complain to them that the carts are left on the wards too long, and that's why they've been pickin' them up when they do."

"Okay, I'll tell Bagley," Mathilda said, leading Laurie into the employees' lounge. Laurie hadn't really understood the man's complaint, but she could tell that Mathilda was very much in charge, and took some pleasure in listening to his problems, knowing she would be instrumental in helping him out.

They proceeded through one of the 'up' wards into the adjoining dining room, where the only sound in the otherwise deadly quiet room was of large spoons hitting metal trays.

"This is the segregated all-male dinin' room," Mathilda said. "The men come down here from the other floors. Bagley likes to have us 'trip' the dinin' rooms durin' meals to see that everything is goin' okay, and to make sure the 'help' don't eat off the cart. I don't say nothin' if I see 'em eatin' after the patients have been fed, but I don't go along with this eatin' before they've fed the patients. The patients ain't so apt to act up either, and the aides don't get to arguin' over who's gonna 'dip' and who's gonna serve, if there's a supervisor around."

After Mathilda introduced Laurie to the psychiatric aides in the male dining room, she showed Laurie another room just off the corridor, that turned out to be the morgue. Using the master key attached to her key cord, she unlocked the door, saying, "I might as well get this part over with as long as we're here."

She and Laurie went into the room, and as Laurie looked around, Mathilda started her little speech -- the same one she had given all the other previous three-to-eleven shift supervisors, most of whom did not remain very long, because... Well, it wasn't quite clear yet to Laurie, and maybe it didn't signify anything in particular. On the other hand, maybe it did.

"This is the morgue for the whole Institution," Mathilda was saying. "Only the supervisors are allowed in here. When patients die in the Main Buildin', their bodies are brought here.

"When you admit a body, be sure you sign it in on this sheet over here, and be sure there's a clothin' sheet in duplicate with the belongin's. When you release a body to the undertaker, make sure he signs for the body and the belongin's. Give the undertaker the carbon..."

Laurie opened her eyes for a moment, shivering in the tub and trying to shake the idea out of her head. But as soon as she relaxed again, she could hear Mathilda's voice as plainly as if she were right there in the room.

"...give the undertaker the carbon, and send the original over to the Record Room in the Main Buildin' to be filed with the patient's permanent record.

"Never release any valuables to the undertaker." She looked Laurie straight in the eye, and looked as serious as if she had been explaining a secret and sacred religious ritual to a novitiate.

"The only valuable that can go along with a body is a weddin' ring, and that is tied to the patient's finger. Anything else must be sent over to the Steward's Office, so the family can pick it up."

"And listen, the thermometer on the refrigerator here has got to be checked every shift! If it goes above forty degrees, be sure you call someone from Maintenance right away. There's room for only two bodies in here, and we don't often have more than two to a time. But if you ever have more than two, there's a big walk-in refrigerator in the kitchen. They don't use it for anything much, and there's enough room in there for a stretcher.

"If you do use it, though, be sure you leave a note on it that there's a body in there. Last winter, durin' flu season, we lost quite a few. Three of 'em were from up-country, and the undertakers couldn't pick 'em up until the next day. Well, we had to use that refrigerator in the kitchen, and the next mornin' when one of the kitchen crew came on duty and opened it, he almost had heart failure!

"Also, sometimes the relatives and the State get into an argument over who's gonna pay the undertaker, so we have to keep those bodies longer than usual."

Laurie sat up in the tub, putting her hands up to her face, controlling an impulse to cry, as she continued reliving the afternoon's events...

Closing the door to the morgue, Mathilda said in the blunt way that Laurie would soon become accustomed to, "Whoever planned to put this morgue right here had his head up his rear end. It's impossible to wheel a body down here without comin' through the ward, which doesn't do much for the patients, especially since most of them know they'll never leave here any other way. It's really bad durin' mealtimes, since it doesn't do much for even a normal person's appetite."

"Couldn't it wait until after the meal's over?" Laurie asked, knowing in advance what the answer would be.

"No, because sometimes the undertakers come right along, and we can't keep 'em waitin'."

"No, we can't keep the undertakers waiting," she thought, as Mathilda led her down the corridor into the female dining room. In a small pantry-like area, one aide dipped from a food cart into sectional metal trays while another aide waited to serve. When Laurie was introduced to Doris Pitts, the aide in charge of adjoining ward A-l, she said hello to this large, dark-haired middle-aged woman who answered her in a soft voice.

On their way up the back stairs to A-3, Mathilda explained to Laurie that Doris Pitts had been in charge of A-l ever since the Annex was built a decade earlier.

"The other aides take their turns at bein' rotated to the difficult wards," Mathilda said, "but Pitts don't. A-l is the easiest ward in the Annex. The patients mostly do everything for themselves and even do a lot of the ward chores."

She hesitated a moment, as if she were deciding whether or not to speak her mind honestly. Then she said, "I've always heard that she has somethin' on the 'higher-ups', and I don't know what it is, but it must be pretty good. Anyway, you're not to move Pitts."

They arrived on A-3 in time to see the first elevator load of female patients returning from the dining room downstairs. Laurie's heart ached as she watched the vacant, unspeaking, robot-like figures make their way to their beds and rocking chairs, with faces devoid of human expression.

And it wasn't any better on the top floor, on A-5, where male patients were lined up, alongside their beds, sitting in rockers; doing nothing, saying nothing, they blended in easily with the ward's furnishings. "What a barren existence," Laurie thought, "for these shells of human beings."

She wondered if anything could ever be done to bring them out, but sensed that they had probably withdrawn many years before. They passed the tub room which at least seemed fairly private, having only two tubs in it. Laurie noticed a large cabinet in one corner, with its open door exposing several rows of bundles of gray material, neatly rolled and fastened with large pins.

"What are those?" she asked.

"Oh, those are bath bundles," Mathilda explained. "Each bundle is a full set of clothin'. The three-to-eleven 'help' make them up in advance, and then they're all ready to be passed out to the patients when they have their weekly baths. Some have to have them made up nightly, because they're so untidy."

"So untidy," Laurie thought, "like infants who can't help themselves."

As they walked through another hallway into A-6, Laurie noticed a patient sitting on a seatless toilet in the doorless patients' bathroom.

"Why aren't there any doors on the bathroom?" Laurie asked, speaking out almost against her better judgment.

"There never have been doors on the bathrooms," Mathilda said.

"So there never will be," Laurie muttered under her breath.

"What did you say?"

"Nothing. Nothing at all."

Continuing the tour, they passed through an adjoining hallway to the 'bed side' and entered A-10. Laurie's horror continued as she watched neat rows of bodies being cared for in assembly-line fashion. She saw a group of aides scurrying about to complete the work for which there was neither enough time nor staff. A large laundry cart occupied the center of ward A-10. The cart was well-stocked with supplies required to do the patient 'changes'-- face cloths and towels, soap and water, bed linen, baby powder, deodorant and combs. Some of the aides were removing supplies from the cart, while others were dumping soiled laundry into the laundry baskets on wheels, pulling them from bed to bed.

Mathilda Hoxie was very proud of Annex's 'bedsore record'.

"We turn 'em three times a shift," she said. "Otherwise we'd have a lot of bed sores. We do have a few, though. We've tried everything, but we can't seem to clear 'em up."

As they started down the stairs to return to the Supervisor's Office, Laurie decided to ask Mathilda why there had been so many other three-to-eleven shift supervisors, and why they had left.

"Ah," Mathilda said, breathing quickly as if the physical effort of walking up and down the stairs were too much for her, "the reason is...the reason is they all tried takin' too much on themselves, and stickin' their noses in where they didn't belong."

When Laurie didn't seem to respond, Mathilda continued. "Bagley don't like no one doin' things on their own. She expects the supervisors to do as she says and to call her if anything comes up. She's hated every RN that's ever come over here, so you better not be startin' anything on your own, or you won't last very long. Bagley likes you to write her little notes about what goes on three to eleven."

As Laurie followed Mathilda Hoxie down the stairs and out through the lobby door to the Supervisor's Office, she thought, "I'll bet there isn't much that goes on around here that Bagley doesn't know about, with Mathilda's eyes to see with and Mathilda's ears to hear with."

Lula Bagley, Annex Chief Supervisor, took Laurie around to the remaining bed wards on the following day. A patient had had an insulin reaction, and Bagley wanted to see if it had been properly written up on the patient's record.

As soon as she read the chart, she started yelling at the young aide in charge, oblivious to Laurie and to the other aides assigned to the ward.

"You have written on this record that the patient had an insulin reaction."

"Is that wrong?" the aide asked.

"Yes, that's wrong," Bagley answered. "Haven't you learned that only a doctor can make a diagnosis?"

"Yes," the aide began, "but..."

"There are no buts about it, lady."

"Then what should I have written?" asked the young aide.

Bagley sighed with impatience, apparently unwilling to go over the same explanation again, as she must have done many times in the past. But she proceeded.

"When you state that a patient has had an insulin reaction, then you are making a diagnosis. How did the patient look, and how did she act?"

"She was very pale and sweaty, and was very restless and staggering around," the young woman said. "This aide is perhaps too intelligent for her own good," Laurie thought, "'takin' too much upon herself,' as Mathilda would have put it."

"All right, then that's what you put on the record!" Bagley yelled.

"Do you realize what legal implications a thing like this could have? This record is a legal document. If it ever had to go to court, we'd really be in the soup!"

They left the aide, blushing with embarrassment, and Bagley turned to Laurie and said, "You know, Canaday, you have to keep tellin' these aides over and over. We keep tellin' 'em how to write these things up, but you have to keep tellin' 'em and tellin' 'em."

"Listen, let me tell you somethin' else. You're not to let any of these aides go home sick without bein' cleared by the duty doctor.

"They'll try to pull that on you, and they'll play one supervisor against the other. If they ask your permission for anything, you tell 'em you'll have to check with Mrs. Bagley. I'm always available, so call me at home any time."

With that last bit of advice, Laurie Canaday was to spend the evening working with Mathilda Hoxie. And from that night on, her orientation would be over and she would be on her own.

CHAPTER FOUR

When Laurie met Dr. Peter Mezummi, she wondered if she should call him "Doctor" at all. He was one of the unlicensed doctors working at Dunton, and he reminded her of a raven, with black hair and black eyes, the kind of bird of prey who would swoop down on his victim and carry her away in his claws.

On her first afternoon of duty on her own, she needed to get an order for an increase in a terminal patient's medication, since he was in a lot of pain and his medication wasn't holding him. Dr. Mezummi met her on the ward, and after they had checked the patient, Dr. Mezummi followed Laurie into the chart room, where she needed to write on the nurse's notes and find the doctor's order sheet. When she sat down, he sat down next to her -- very close to her -- and started rubbing his leg against hers.

She moved her chair, and he moved his. When she moved her chair again, he did the same. By this time, she was in a corner, so she eased herself to her feet, and left the room. As she was walking down the stairs with him on his way out, he forced his way in front of her and turned around, so that he was standing on a lower step.

"I wonder how much you weigh," he said, grabbing her under the arms and picking her up.

"Put me down!" she yelled.

"Ah, you're heavier than I thought," he said, lowering her back to her feet and holding her so close that she had to rub against him on her way down.

"He is more than living up to his reputation as a skirt-chaser," Laurie thought. She was so taken with the image of a raven, that she could almost hear his wings fluttering as he flew away.

Laurie stood motionless on the stairway for a moment, trying to regain her composure. She didn't want any of the aides to see her this way -- angry, her feelings wounded, and her pride tarnished.

Later she noticed that a ten-to-six aide had been assigned to a slower bed ward, when another bed ward was much busier; she sent the young woman to the busier ward.

"By the way," complained the aide, "Why have I been rotated back to these shit wards so soon? It's not my turn. I've been moved half a dozen times, while Pitts hasn't had to move at all! What's she got on these people anyway?"

"I don't know," Laurie said, "but I bet it would be very interesting to find out."

Laurie hadn't realized what a big mistake she'd made until the following afternoon. Lula Bagley descended on her, having lost all of her cool exterior, and yelling like a banshee.

"What's the big idea movin' the ten-to-six aide off A-11? Who gave you orders to do that?"

Laurie was almost too shocked to speak, but managed to get a few words out. "A-10 was much busier, so I thought..."

"Thought?" Bagley said. "Were you hired to think, or were you hired to follow my orders? A-11 has always had a ten-to-six girl, so please don't be takin' things upon yourself again, no matter what you think."

For whatever reasons, if there were any reasons at all, Lula Bagley was fighting to keep the status quo, and no new nurse was going to come around and change things -- not while Lula Bagley was in charge!

Laurie was appalled the very next night when it turned out that she would have to cover for the male-side supervisor who had called in sick. Mathilda Hoxie didn't like working in the Main Building, so she would work in Laurie's place at the Annex, as Grace Maybury explained.

Laurie had another one of those strange feelings, as if something terrible were going to happen, but she wasn't in a position to say no, so she walked over to report for work.

As she was 'tripping' one of the wards, she heard the male-side supervisor being paged.

"Uh-oh," she thought. "That's me!"

When she picked up the phone, the operator told her that a male patient had just cut his wrists. "Oh, God," she thought, running to the ward and seeing a patient in the dimly-lit chart room with two attendants pressing four-by-fours to the cuts on both of his wrists.

"Please help me," she heard him saying, and she knew right away that it was Perley.

As she went to stand at his side, she asked the attendant to page the doctor on call. There was so much bleeding that she knew sutures would be required.

"How did this happen?" she asked the attendant.

"He smashed the window with his shoe and cut his wrists with the glass."

Laurie planted both of her feet on the floor, to keep herself from trembling. Then she looked into his eyes, and said, "Why did you do it, Perley?"

He didn't know her; he didn't even seem to wonder how she had known his name. He just said, "I don't want to live anymore, and yet I can't die. All I'm going to do is keep falling and falling forever into a bottomless pit."

"We're here to help you, Perley," she said. When she heard footsteps behind her, she turned to see Dr. Salvatore Gallino, tall and straight, with every gray hair in place, come into the ward. Then she was all business, getting the suture tray from the dressing cart, unfolding a package of sterile gloves, and placing them in front of Dr. Gallino.

As the attendant brought in a small table for Perley to put his arms on, and an apron for the doctor to protect his clothing, Dr. Gallino started telling Laurie what a famous surgeon he had been in Europe. "I'm always happy to use my surgical skills, and even if I do say so myself, I'm a cut above the other physicians here. And they know it."

Then he asked, "Do you have any triple-0 chromic?"

Using transfer forceps, Laurie removed one of the suture paks from a large bottle filled with solution. Dr. Gallino, holding a gauze sponge in each hand to protect his gloves from being cut, broke the glass tube and shook the suture onto the tray. Then, grasping a needle holder, he clicked the horseshoe-shaped needle into place and began to thread it.

"Be real still now, Perley," Laurie said to him, leaning down close to his face. "I'm going to cleanse your cuts and paint them with Mercressin so you won't get an infection." She always liked telling the patients what she was doing, so they wouldn't be afraid. But Perley just stared at her, as if he didn't even see her.

After draping Perley's arm with a sterile towel from the tray, Dr. Gallino put the point of the needle to Perley's flesh.

"Wouldn't you like to use some anesthetic?" Laurie said to him. "We have Ethanol here, if you'd like to spray some on."

"Never mind that," the doctor said. "We don't need anesthesia, with patients like these. These people don't feel pain."

And then Dr. Gallino proved his point, as Laurie cringed, watching the minor operation in amazement and horror. But it was true; Perley sat without flinching while the doctor applied five sutures to each wrist. "He must be very far gone," Laurie thought, and the expression "out of his mind" suddenly took on a new meaning for her, since he was past the point of caring about his own misery.

Laurie put a sterile dressing on Perley's wrists and told the attendant that she would walk him back to his bed.

"Call someone from Maintenance right away to take care of the broken glass and to cover the window," she said.

Helping Perley to stand and putting his arm through hers, she remembered how often they had walked together, arm in arm, in the days of their sweet youth. But they weren't walking in a garden in the moonlight, and they weren't walking on the beach on a late summer afternoon. They were walking as nurse and patient, down the shining, highly-polished floor of a mental institution, after the patient had tried to commit suicide.

He may not have known her name, but when they got to his bed and she had helped him to lie down, he said, "Will you stay with me until I fall asleep?"

"Yes, of course," Laurie said, wondering if she would be getting herself in hot water with Grace Maybury, wasting her time sitting with a sick man, and keeping him company for a little while, just until he fell asleep. She had learned from the aides that Grace Maybury had always told them, "If you're talking with a patient, you'd better have a mop in your hand."

Perley didn't speak for a long time, but then he said, "I'm afraid, Nurse."

"Afraid of what, Perley?"

He couldn't answer her, and seemed to be groping around for the reasons. And Laurie hoped that he might remember who she was after a while, but it didn't seem possible. So she decided that if he didn't recognize her face or the sound of her voice, at least she would be happy if he recognized her genuine concern about him, as one human being to another.

Finally he said, "I'm afraid that when I die, I'll fall into a bottomless pit and keep falling and falling forever and ever."

Then he started breathing deeply and rhythmically, and when he fell asleep, Laurie got up as quietly as she could and returned to the Supervisor's Office.

She hoped that she had been some small comfort to Perley in what must have been one of the darkest hours of his life.

The following evening, Laurie had a second encounter with Dr. Gallino that confirmed her poor opinion of him. When a young aide working on A-8 found patient Addie Green dead in her bed, she had Laurie paged immediately, saying the death was sudden, since the patient hadn't had any apparent problems. Laurie went to the ward to examine the patient, and then notified the duty doctor to come over to pronounce the patient expired. A few minutes later, Dr. Gallino showed up, looking all around him and turning his nose up at what he saw.

"Just look at all these useless bodies here. I'd like to take some chloroform around and put them all to sleep permanently."

"Why did you ever become a doctor?" Laurie thought, handing him a stethoscope to listen for any heart sounds, and a flashlight to check the patient's pupils for reaction to light.

"I wonder if maybe you're not just a plumber or a brick layer in disguise. Famous surgeon, my foot!"

"Probable coronary," he muttered, making the proper notations on the patient's diagnosis card, and then returning to the Main Building to notify the next of kin of her death.

Since Laurie hadn't been working at Dunton long enough to be familiar with all the patients' names, she wasn't aware that there were, in fact, two Addie Greens. And if she had known it, she might have warned Dr. Gallino and saved the Institution and the families of both Addie Greens a great deal of anguish.

The next afternoon, when Laurie reported for duty, Lula Bagley wasn't in her office as usual. She was on A-8, the ward where Addie Green had died, and she was screaming her head off at the young aide who had found the body.

"Don't you know that you must never put on a patient's notes that she has expired? Didn't you ever hear of the word, 'appears'? From now on, when you write up a report, you put down that the patient appears to have expired. How many times do I have to tell you that only the doctor can pronounce a patient dead. Do you understand that, Ames?" She didn't wait for the aide to answer, but stormed right ahead.

"You'll have to do this sheet all over again. You can't send it over like this. The shit would hit the fan!"

Then Bagley turned, and seeing Laurie, began shouting at her.

"And you, Canaday, you had the undertaker sign one copy of the clothing record, and he took it with him. He could have lost the whole kit and caboodle, and where would that have left us? You always make out the clothing record in duplicate. Then we have something . As it is right now, we don't have a damn thing to show that we released all those belongings. The trouble you could have gotten us into."

The trouble that Laurie could have gotten them into was nothing compared to the trouble they were already in.

Addie Green's sister, Mrs. Sarah Finch, was an old woman who lived three hours away from Dunton. Since she couldn't drive by herself, she hadn't been able to visit Addie in over ten years. Now, she made the trip with one of her sons, making all the necessary arrangements with a local funeral director, since she thought it would be just as easy to have Addie waked where she was, and then transport her body to the family burial plot near her home.

At the wake, Mrs. Finch couldn't get over how much her sister had changed. As she later told the story, her sister looked like an altogether different person.

"Your eyesight has really gone downhill," everyone kept reminding her. But still she thought that Addie had changed an awful lot -- even for ten years.

On the third day after Addie's death, her body began its three-hour trip to the family burial plot.

That same morning, Martha Linscott, the aide in charge of A-8 nearly fainted when she answered a knock on the door.

"Uh, I think you'd better come with me to the office, Ma'am," she said.

"Come to the office? Why? What's the matter?" Addie Green's daughter said, but Martha was too afraid to speak, and waited for Lula Bagley to give this woman the sad news that her mother was dead.

"Mrs. Bagley," Martha said, opening the office door and showing the woman in, "this is Addie Green's daughter, and she's here to visit her mother."

"What?" Bagley exclaimed, getting up from her chair and practically knocking it over. "You mean you weren't notified of your mother's death?"

"My mother's death?" screamed the daughter, falling into the nearest chair.

"Your mother died three days ago, and we -- naturally -- assumed that you had been notified. I'll call Mrs. Maybury, the Director of Nurses, and Dr. Atherton, the Superintendent."

No one had yet said they were sorry. Martha Linscott felt terrible, and wanted to take the woman's hand, but was too ashamed and mortified even to speak.

Dr. Atherton greeted the woman warmly, trying to make her as comfortable as possible. As soon as Dr. Gallino arrived, shame-faced for being called on the carpet, Dr. Atherton said, "Didn't you notify the family of the patient's death?"

"Yes, of course I did."

"Well, this is Mrs. Green's daughter, and she knew nothing about it."

"I'm terribly...that is, I'm so sorry," Dr. Gallino said.

Then Dr. Atherton took him and Lula Bagley to the Record Room and discovered that there were two records with the name Addie Green, and that the wrong Addie Green's family had been notified.

"Then Mrs. Green's sister -- that is, Mrs. Finch -- is burying the wrong..." Lula Bagley began, and Dr. Atherton said, "Get in touch with the Bonville family right away!"

While Addie Green's daughter waited, they called the undertaker who reported that the body was already on its way to the burial plot. The hearse was apparently on the Interstate, heading south.

"Then call the State Police," Dr. Atherton said, "and instruct them to overtake the hearse and have the driver return here, or else they'll be burying the wrong body."

Addie Green's daughter suddenly burst out crying, sobbing uncontrollably, and Dr. Atherton went to her side to console her. As Grace Maybury later told the story, the State Police car entered the cemetery just as the presiding priest was saying his graveside prayers.

"What is this all about?" Mrs. Finch asked.

"There has been some sort of mix-up," the policeman said, with his hat in his hand. "My instructions are to tell the driver of this hearse to bring the body back where he got it, and to bring you back to Dunton State Mental Institution."

"Some sort of mix-up?" Mrs. Finch said. "I don't understand."

"This is not your sister's body," the policeman said. "That's all I know."

When Mrs. Finch was brought into Dr. Atherton's office, she still wasn't sure whether her sister was dead or alive, but when it was all explained to her, she said, "I knew there was something strange about the way that woman looked. I mean, I seemed to be the only one who didn't think she could possibly by my sister!"

Then Dr. Atherton turned to Addie Green's daughter -- that is, the Addie Green who was actually dead, and said, "I can't tell you how sorry I am that this has happened."

And to Mrs. Finch, he said, "I can't undo the harm that has already been done. All I can do is to offer to compensate you -- both of you, for all the pain and anguish you have suffered."

Although Grace Maybury wasn't privileged with the exact amount of their settlement, she knew that it was agreeable to all, and the two injured parties left, one of them sadder, but both of them somewhat richer for their troubles.

"It could have turned into a nice little scandal," Maybury said to Bagley, after they returned to Maybury's office.

Later, after Bagley had reported the incident to Mathilda Courtland, she was heard to say, "Gallino could have been fired on the spot, but he's Atherton's fair-haired boy. Can you just imagine the State Police chasing that hearse around, with the wrong body in it? If the newspaper ever got hold of that, they'd sure have a field day."

CHAPTER FIVE

Laurie had been making friends with Sharon Lovejoy, the young nurse she had met on her first day of duty at Dunton. Although they were assigned to different buildings and hours, they sometimes met for supper in the employees' dining room, commonly known as EDR, located in the Main Building.

One evening, Sharon confided to Laurie that she had been approached regarding reassignment to the male violent ward, due to suspicions of abuse taking place on that ward.

"I've heard that they've never allowed a woman to set foot up there," said Laurie, surprisedly.

"I know," agreed Sharon, "and I do have concerns, but I've decided to accept the challenge."

"Good for you!" said Laurie. "I'm sure you'll be able to make a difference."

Then Sharon began telling Laurie about one of her patients, Perley Graves.

"He hadn't been eating or drinking for three days, so I called Dr. Gallino in, and told him that Perley was the patient who had slashed his wrists. Gallino asked me to bring him a gastric tray, a No. 20 Levine tube, and some Sustagen. It made me cringe, Laurie, because I knew what was coming."

Laurie dreaded to hear what Sharon was about to tell her, and was thankful that she had not been the one to assist in that procedure.

"Perley kept saying that he didn't want to be fed," Sharon continued, "and that he wanted to die, but Gallino wouldn't listen. When he tried inserting the tube into Perley's nostril, Perley started pulling at it, so Gallino called over two attendants to hold him down while he forced that large tube through his nose and down his throat. Perley wouldn't swallow so the tube could pass easily, but Gallino kept pushing it down anyway. Blood started oozing from Perley's mouth. That tube must have been shredding his membranes."

Sharon paused to blow a thin stream of air out of her mouth, exhaling it like a whistle. "And then Gallino started pushing in the liquid nourishment as fast as he could. Poor Perley kept vomiting it, but Gallino kept on pushing it down. I felt like a criminal even being there."

"But it was not your fault," Laurie said, trying to make Sharon feel better.

"Gallino used such a large Levine tube that it seemed to me that he wanted to torture Perley. I even asked him if he'd intentionally wanted to hurt Perley. And do you know what he said? He said, 'Yes, because if I hurt him enough, he'll remember, and won't pull it out, and I won't have to do this again.' By the way, he's written the order for Perley to be transferred to the Annex."

Laurie was happy to hear that Perley would now be under her care, but she did not look forward to seeing him in such a horrible condition.

"He just wants to die," she kept thinking, but in the back of her mind she was hoping that she could think of some way to give him a reason to want to live again.

The next time Laurie saw Perley, after his transfer to the Annex, he did seem to remember that he'd seen her before, but couldn't say when. Laurie didn't want to tell him that it was on the night he'd tried to kill himself, and she thought she'd talk about something cheerful, something completely innocuous like the weather, or the baseball season, since she remembered that he'd been a star pitcher for their high school team.

But Perley didn't want to talk about baseball, and Laurie began to realize that her job of consoling him would not be easy. He was obsessed with fear that when he died, he would just keep falling into a bottomless pit -- would just keep falling into it forever, without end.

"But death isn't like that at all," Laurie said, sitting on a chair near his bed and trying to speak in a low voice so she wouldn't disturb any of the other patients.

"Death is the beginning of a peaceful, happy life that goes on forever," she said, trying to allay his fears.

"How do you know?" he said, sounding more hurt than angry. "How could you possibly know about death?" He turned his face away from her as he had done before, and wouldn't speak again. It must have been hard for him to speak in any case, with the stub hanging out of his nose like some grotesque growth coming from inside his body.

She sat with him a little while longer, without speaking, and wondered if she could arrange a visit to Perley from the staff psychologist. After all, this was supposed to be a mental institution, and the patients were entitled to psychological care as well as physical care, weren't they? Yes, she would ask about getting Perley a session with Randy Sinclair. Then maybe he would begin to improve. Then maybe he would regain his memory of his own past.

Since Laurie hardly ever saw Dr. Atherton, she didn't know until her first month at Dunton that he lived in a beautiful apartment on the top floor of the Main Building with his wife. Mrs. Atherton was a mysterious woman who hardly ever left the Institution, except to be driven into town to do her shopping every few days. Dr. Atherton had hired a man named Jake to be Mrs. Atherton's chauffeur, and it was common knowledge that she was "strange, and as nutty as a fruitcake."

So when Hannah Simpson, one of the older, more motherly aides, was called to report to duty at the Atherton's apartment, it was assumed that *Mrs.* Atherton had finally "gone off her rocker", as Mathilda Courtland put it. But Mathilda and everyone else were in for a big surprise when Hannah came down at the end of the day and reported that it was *Dr.* Atherton and not his wife who needed her care.

"He's still got that old cigar in his mouth , but he can hardly stand up," she said to Grace Maybury, who'd been working with the good doctor for more than a decade, basking in his power and glory.

"What's wrong with him, Hannah?" she said. "Is he going to be all right, or is it serious?"

Hannah bit her lower lip as she thought these questions over, and then she said, "I could almost see him getting weaker right before my eyes. I think he's...I think he's going to die, Mrs. Maybury. Dr. Bahai came up to examine him -- in private, mind you, making me leave the room as if there were some great secret ceremony going on -- but when he came out, he just shook his head. 'He may have a week left, or maybe just a day or two,' he said, and that was that."

"Jesus, Mary, and Joseph!" Grace Maybury exclaimed, getting up to pace her office floor, wondering out loud how in the world she would survive without Dr. Atherton. Another superintendent would never give her such support.

"And what'll I do if Bahai takes his place?" she said. "He and I have had our horns locked for the past ten years. He'll just eat me alive if he takes over! He'll fry me and serve me up for lunch. There's no doubt about it!"

The next morning, Dr. Bahai came downstairs to break the news that Dr. Atherton was dead. He had died quietly during the night, and his wife had sat up with his body, wanting to be alone with him for a while before she would be made to leave the Institution. She didn't even have a home to go to, but her husband had left detailed instructions to be carried out in the event of his death. The first request was that Grace Maybury see to it that Mrs. Atherton be placed in a private mental institution.

"Ha, he certainly wouldn't have put her in here!" she said, reading through the doctor's instructions. "But he's made enough money at Dunton, and saved enough by not having to pay for any of his expenses, to put his wife in the most expensive hospital in the country!"

The way Lula Bagley talked about it, Maybury was angry at Dr. Atherton for dying and leaving her. But she soon got over her anger, and began to prepare herself for his successor.

According to Dr. Atherton's wishes, no formal observance was made of his death. Bagley told Laurie that that was the way he wanted it.

"Dr. Atherton believed that when you're dead, you're dead, and asked that we tell everybody to refrain from sending flowers or cards or anything sentimental. There'll be no services or wake of any kind, and he just wanted us to go on with our work, as if nothing had happened, since, as he always said, 'the patients come first'."

How sad," Laurie said, "not to stop for a moment and recognize the man for what he accomplished."

"Dr. Atherton did accomplish a great deal," Lula Bagley said. Mrs. Maybury is sure gonna miss him. He ran a tight ship here.

We're all worried about what's gonna happen now that he's gone."

Laurie wondered too, but never could she have imagined the critical state of affairs that was to follow.

On a shared day off, Laurie invited her friend Sharon to her home for lunch. Even though they started their discussion with some small talk, they ended up talking about their jobs, since nursing was a primary part of their lives.

And now they had a lot to talk about.

The Institution seemed to be up for grabs -- no longer insulated against 'outside' interference now that Dr. Atherton was gone. They spoke about the leaflets they had recently seen on all the wards -- union leaflets from the AFSCME and the AFL-CIO.

"Bagley told me that the unions have been trying to worm their way in for years, but Dr. Atherton kept them out, and she's afraid of them," Sharon said, walking around the living room and looking at a group of photographs up over the mantelpiece. She found some pictures of Laurie as a girl with her parents, and with a group of friends, and she stopped for a moment, staring at a picture of someone who seemed vaguely familiar to her, although she didn't make any connection with Perley Graves, since the boy looked so happy and carefree.

Laurie had set the serving tray down on the coffee table, and said, "Cream and sugar?"

"I'll get my own, thank you," Sharon said, coming to sit down across from Laurie, and taking a few good-looking, homemade cookies on her plate. "Did you bake these?"

"Oh, no," Laurie said, laughing. "You know I'd never have time to do any baking. My mom did. She's the best cookie-maker on the block."

The young women sipped their coffee, thinking of many things and trying to distill their thoughts down to the one, most important issue.

"Maybury calls the union representatives 'vultures'," Sharon said, "because they're trying to organize the aides, and you know what a disaster that would be."

"A disaster?" Laurie said. "It's about time someone did something for those poor aides. I overheard the union man saying he could get them a forty-hour work week, so I'm pretty sure the union will be voted in. Besides, now the aides will have somebody to complain to when Bagley or Maybury starts screaming at them.

"The representative said they'd supply someone to walk into Maybury's office with them if they wanted to file a grievance, and that they can't be forced to work a double shift anymore."

"Poor Maybury, she won't be able to intimidate the union stewards! She won't know what to do."

"Oh, I don't feel sorry for her," Sharon said, looking back up at the mantelpiece again. "You know, there's someone in that group portrait who looks familiar to me. Is that your graduating class?"

"Yes," Laurie said. "Which one do you think you've seen before?"

"The tall, blonde kid. He's got a sparkle in his eyes that reminds me of...I don't know. His name is on the tip of my tongue somehow, but I can't seem to spit it out."

"It's Perley Graves," Laurie whispered, but Sharon had heard her and said, "The same Perley Graves who -- who tried to kill himself?"

Laurie put down her cup and said, "Yes, and there aren't two of him the way there were two Addie Greens."

"I didn't know you knew him!"

Laurie looked down at her lap and wiped a crumb off her skirt.

"I knew him, yes. But he's hardly the same person anymore. I don't even know what's been going on in his life all these years. When I went away to college, we wrote to each other at first. But you know how it is when you go away. You get so involved with other things, meeting other people, that you can't just keep thinking about the boy you left behind.

"I thought that maybe he'd improve a bit, if he could get a chance to see a psychologist, and I even had a visit set up for him with Randy Sinclair. But apparently, they just sat and stared out the window the whole time."

"It's always been difficult getting Randy to visit with a male patient," Sharon said, disgustedly. "On the other hand, he is more than willing to give 'therapy' to a female patient, especially if she is pretty and under twenty. It gives me the creeps, and I'm sorry to hear about Perley. It's too bad there's no one else for him to talk to."

"I'll try to talk to him myself," Laurie thought, wondering if she could possibly help Perley when no one else could.

CHAPTER SIX

One by one, they started calling in -- the aides assigned to the various wards on the eleven-to-seven shift on the Saturday night of the big snow storm. As Laurie answered the first of many phone calls that night, Paula Breton was saying, "There's no way I can get in to work. I managed to get my car out of my driveway, but just up the street the snow drifts are so high that I had to go straight back home."

"I can't understand it," Laurie said. "The weatherman didn't say anything about a tremendous snow storm, but I can see that it's amounting to a lot more than the 'flurries' they predicted this morning. Anyway, don't worry about it, Paula. Come in as soon as it's safe to do so."

"Now, what am I going to do without Paula?" she thought, when she heard her name being paged again.

This time, it was Evelyn Davis. "I hate to have to tell you this, Miss Canaday," she said, "but I'm still at home. We've lost our power, and I'm going to have to stay here to help my husband keep watch over the wood fire, so that we can keep this place from freezing."

"Well, don't worry," Laurie said, trying to sound as reassuring as possible. "That should certainly be your first concern. We'll manage somehow."

After four consecutive absent calls, Laurie wondered how they *would* manage. An outbreak of flu in the Annex during the past few days was beginning to reach epidemic proportions. They had lost two patients already, one this morning , and one the day before, neither of whose remains had yet been picked up.

"Now, the undertakers won't be able to get here either," she was thinking. "What a time for a snow storm, with so many patients sick with the flu!"

Laurie set about the unpleasant task of telling her staff that they wouldn't be relieved that night, and therefore wouldn't be able to leave their posts. She couldn't have known then, nor could they, that they would all be trapped in the Annex for *three* nights, cut off from the outside world by the worst storm in area history.

"I don't think we'd get very far anyway, if you let us go," said an A-8 aide, straining to see through a window into the darkness. Snow was piling up beyond the window, and the drifts jutting in the air told them that this was no ordinary storm.

"Maggie Gallagher isn't doing well at all," one of the aides rushed up to report. "I don't think she's gonna last much longer."

As Laurie accompanied the aide to the patient's bedside, she said, "She's certainly gone downhill fast. She looks a lot worse than she did even a few hours ago. This is a very potent strain of virus, and it seems to be hitting them hard. Dr. Bauer said there's nothing we can do for them except to force fluids, and try to keep them comfortable."

Dr. Herman Bauer, the Annex physician, was one of the only staff doctors that Laurie felt any friendship for. He was an older man, with a heavy German accent, and although he seemed inept at times, at least he had a fatherly way of dealing with the patients and the staff, and he was very well liked.

Laurie was beginning to wish he could come over and 'trip' the Annex wards with her. It was already fifteen minutes past the time when the next supervisor, Nurse June Buck was supposed to relieve her. Buck's four-wheel drive Land Rover had seen her to work through many a storm. But Laurie hadn't even heard from her yet, so it seemed plausible that Buck was stuck somewhere in the snow, and couldn't even reach a phone to call in that she'd be late.

Worried that Buck might be stranded, Laurie decided to try to call her, but when she picked up the receiver, all she heard was an ominous buzzing.

"Oh, no, the lines are down," she thought, fearfully, realizing that the winds were so strong -- reaching hurricane force, as she later learned -- that they were tearing down telephone lines throughout the area.

On A-4, the patients were beginning to show their fear of the howling wind outside their windows.

"We can't see anything," they said, peering out but seeing only the blank wall of snow outside. Laurie and an aide tried their best to comfort the patients, but they were beginning to show signs of their own fear, since by now it was obvious to everyone that they were cut off -- entombed in the Annex -- with no way to get out, and no way for anyone else to get in.

Laurie ran back through A-4 to A-8, where two staff were on duty.

"Grab the push brooms and put on your coat and boots," she yelled to one of them. "We've got to try clearing the front entranceway. For whatever it's worth, we have to have at least one way in and out of here!"

After getting fully dressed with coats and boots, Laurie and the aide tried in vain to battle against the raging snow and sub-zero temperatures. But the freezing wind cut into their faces and fingers, drifting back into the small cleared exit as quickly as they could clear it.

For the next fifty-six hours, the Annex staff would work relentlessly, aide after aide taking turn after turn at this continuous effort, while in the town of Somerset below, emergency highway crews would battle through snow-drifts twenty feet high. With winds up to twenty knots dumping snow on the roads as quickly as they were cleared, thousands of vehicles were either buried or ditched, and hundreds of people were left stranded.

Since the paging system was now out of commission, Laurie had to keep moving throughout the wards to see how the patients and staff were holding up, trying to spread whatever little cheer she could manage to summon. On her third trip to A-8, she found that Maggie Gallagher had indeed died.

Laurie had known it would happen, but hadn't wanted to think about it, knowing as she did that the morgue was already fully occupied with the two already deceased patients. After going down to the drug room to procure a morgue pack, Laurie wrapped Maggie's body and labeled it, realizing that there was only one place for it now. She wrote a note to attach to the door of the walk-in refrigerator, remembering what Mathilda Courtland had told her during her orientation...

..."We had to use that walk-in refrigerator in the kitchen, and the next day, when the kitchen crew came on duty and opened it, they almost had heart failure!"...

Laurie and an aide quickly placed the body on a stretcher, wheeled it to the elevator, and took it to the basement kitchen.

"There are lots of other really sick patients, Miss Canaday," the aide said with a worried tone in her voice. "What will we do if any more of them die?"

"I don't know," Laurie said, "I really don't know what we would do."

"What we're *going* to do," she thought, knowing quite well that more patients would be dying, especially if there was no help from the outside. They would be able to feed the patients for a day or two, with the remaining food supply, but if the pipes froze and they had no water... If the furnace went out and they had no heat...

She shivered involuntarily at the thought. No, it *wouldn't* happen. It *couldn't* happen.

But if it did, she would be prepared!

The gray dawn of Sunday brought the exhausted workers no relief staff, but they continued to push forward, while in Somerset, plow crews were operating around the clock to dig the area out of this avalanche of snow and rescue any stranded survivors. Now Laurie had to think of food , but since the dietary crew had left the evening before, while the roads were still passable, she and the aides would have to prepare any food they found, by themselves.

"There might not even be any food left," Laurie was thinking on her way to the kitchen. At first, she found nothing at all. But by the grace of God, tucked away in one of the back cupboards, she came across a huge supply of oatmeal.

"Well, at least there's enough oatmeal here to see us through the storm," she thought. Years later, she was still unable to eat it without remembering exactly how it felt during that terrible ordeal. It always made her shiver just to remember it, but the oatmeal she found would keep them all from starving. She then decided what their next course of action would be.

To her A-2 aide, she said, "I'm going to use a stretcher to deliver this oatmeal throughout the wards. I don't know how long we're going to be in this situation, so as of right now, we're going to concern ourselves only with the bare necessities, and I do mean, the BARE NECESSITIES."

"It doesn't matter if the cleaning doesn't get done, or if the beds don't get made. Just keep the patients fed, medicated, and comfortable. After you've done that, find a spare bed and get some rest. I'm going to ask the girl on A-1 to 'trip' both of these wards. When you've had some sleep, you can do the same for her. I don't want any bed linen changed unless absolutely necessary. Since we won't have any laundry service, we'll have to make due with what we have."

The aide nodded her approval of Laurie's plan.

After delivering food to A-1, Laurie loaded the stretcher with fresh linen for the incontinent patients and distributed it to the appropriate wards. She then returned the stretcher to the kitchen and stacked it with cartons of oatmeal.

Beginning with A-7, the basement ward on the 'bed side', she began her trek throughout the Annex, delivering food, and instructing all of her staff as to the procedure they would be following. She then sank into an empty bed and fell asleep.

Laurie was awakened after a short time by an aide with the news that another patient had died. Still groggy from sleep, she looked up at the ceiling and could hear a hum coming from the lights, which meant that power was coming from the auxiliary source. She wasn't even sure where she was at first, and shot up in bed, opening her eyes wide to find herself back in the Annex, where it seemed she had been for days.

Her uniform wrinkled, and her hair unkempt, she made a second trip to the drug room for a morgue pack before going to A-9.

"Do you have any suggestions about what we can do with Alice?" Laurie asked the aide, after completing Alice's postmortem care.

"How about putting her in the tub room? We certainly won't be giving any baths for a while."

"I'm more concerned with finding a cool place," Laurie said, "but I suppose we could put her in the tub room upstairs on A-11 and open the windows and close the door. The snow is piled high above *these* windows."

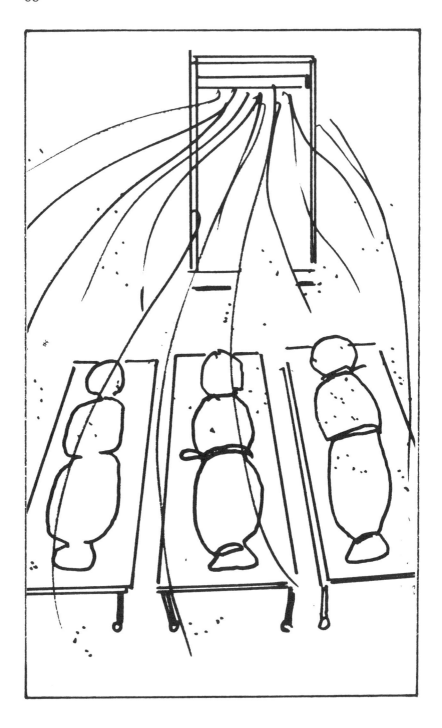

"Well, it'll certainly be cool up there once we open the windows," said the aide. "The snow will just fall in like an avalanche!"

So the top floor, A-ll tub room, became the temporary morgue, and by the time the storm had died out, four more patients had succumbed to the flu, bringing the total to seven.

Wet sheets were being hung over bedposts, linen carts -- anywhere they could dry -- and then being returned to the beds.

The smell on the wards was becoming intolerable. One of the younger aides began crying, saying, "We're trapped. We'll be here forever!" Laurie tried to calm her, reminding her that they had work to do and patients to care for. She helped the young woman drape urine-soaked sheets throughout the ward, reeling with the stench, and beginning to feel the signs of her own exhaustion.

The crew was drained of patience as they approached the third night of the siege. Two more patients died from the flu during that night, their bodies taken up to the makeshift morgue on A-ll, along with the others. The snow had blown fiercely through the opened window, blanketing the bodies in a shroud of snow.

"I wonder how they're managing over at the Main Building," the aide helping Laurie said.

This was the first time Laurie had stopped to think about the others. "Probably somewhat better than we are," she said. "At least they have a supply of food and clean linen."

"I'd give anything right now for a change of clothes," the aide said, "and for a comfortable bed. I'm beginning to smell as bad as the wards, and I'm almost afraid to go to sleep for fear of being suffocated by the stench."

On the morning of the third day, Laurie could hear the distant sounds of a helicopter breaking the silence. The flapping noise of the rotating propeller blades grew louder and louder, until finally the deafening sound told her that it was directly overhead.

Everyone else had heard it too, and soon a crowd had congregated at the windows.

Laurie threw on her coat and boots, and ran outside as fast as her feeble legs would carry her. Some of the others had followed her to watch the hovering Air Force rescue helicopter let down a rope attached to a cable, and begin to lower supplies down to them.

Box after box was brought inside, and the group said a prayer of thanksgiving as they took the ready-to-eat meals from the boxes.

Soon after this, the sounds of a mighty bulldozer could be heard pushing its way up the hill through giant mounds of snow. Everyone's excitement at this welcomed sound was somewhat dampened by the sight of water running out from under the A-ll tub-room door, escaping from a water pipe damaged by the frigid temperature. As the bulldozer did its work, so was the water on the upstairs' floor turning into a river.

Although it took most of the day for the machine to push its way through to them, Laurie was so relieved that she practically fainted when she saw the path leading to the outside world.

When she heard her name being paged, she thought that she was hearing things. But it was actually true; telephone communication had been restored.

"What do you people need most over there?" said the voice from the Main Building.

"A maintenance man and an undertaker," Laurie said. "And I need to speak to Dr. Bauer. He has a lot of families to notify of his patients' deaths that have occurred here, one as long as four days ago."

By late afternoon of that third day, access to the Hill had been restored, and as the relief staff began taking over, the weary captives, one by one, were set free.

PART II

RAVAGE OF A FERTILE FIELD

CHAPTER SEVEN

The Union was voted in by an overwhelming majority. New housekeeping, dietary, clerical and activity staff were hired so that Nursing would no longer have to 'pick up the tab' by performing these duties, along with their own. A great deal of time would now need to be spent correcting violations of fair-labor practices. A whole new work schedule had to be set up to provide a forty-hour work week, and it was beginning to look as if the tables were turning. Now, the 'help' seemed to have the upper hand. And if Dr. Bahai wasn't careful, he could have a revolution on his hands.

Placed almost against his will in the position of Acting Superintendent, Dr. Joseph Bahai, one of the most gentle and compassionate doctors Laurie had ever met, soon found himself to be no match against the opportunists who swooped down upon the Institution, as Grace Maybury had said, like vultures.

Rick Armstrong was one of the first to descend. As a Master's degreed recreational therapist, he felt that it was inequitable for him to be working under a woman with only a Bachelor's degree. Even though he'd been working at Dunton only a year, he insisted that he was more qualified for the job of Head of Recreational Therapy than was Christina Tewksberry, who had held that position for fifteen years under Dr. Atherton.

"You may not like it, Dr. Bahai," Rick said, "but I have just cause for a grievance and you know I can win. You must ask Mrs. Tewksberry to step down."

Dr. Bahai, who had made many friends at Dunton during his long years of service there, felt that his back was up against a wall. When he agreed to allow Rick Armstrong to take over and informed Christina of his decision, she was deeply shocked and hurt, but she said, "I understand your position, Dr. Bahai, but I want you to understand that I could not go on working in that department under Rick Armstrong."

"Then we'll create another position for you, Mrs. Tewksberry," Dr. Bahai said, out of the goodness of his heart.

She then became the Director of Volunteers, doing a fine job of soliciting ladies' and church groups to do shopping for the patients, make curtains and drapes for bare windows, make up Christmas packages to distribute throughout the wards, and perform many other worthwhile functions.

Unfortunately, Rick Armstrong was failing miserably in his job, and it seemed that in just a few weeks' time, his department had fallen into utter chaos.

It was a difficult fall and winter for Dr. Bahai, who was growing weary of the union's demands and of Grace Maybury's endless whining and moaning.

As he sat in his office, waiting for a new opportunist to arrive for his interview, Dr. Bahai received a phone call from Grace Maybury, complaining that she was short-handed again and needed more help, since no one would work overtime anymore.

"And I can't force them to stay over anymore, like I used to!" she said.

"It must be a terrible disappointment to you," the doctor said, thinking that finally she was getting back some of her own medicine.

"I'm afraid there's nothing I can do," he said, thinking that it would serve her right if she had to work all the overtime hours herself.

When Dr. Bahai looked up to meet psychologist Dr. Zeb Ramsey for the first time, he saw a tall man of about thirty-five enter his office, with long hair and a long, thick beard. Stooping as he approached the desk, Dr. Ramsey held his hand out and shook Dr. Bahai's hand.

"So you're interested in setting up a new program?" Dr. Bahai said, as Dr. Ramsey sat down.

"Yes, sir," said the younger man. "I would like to apply for a federal grant in order to implement a Behavior Modification program on one of your wards. It would be necessary to redistribute some your patients, because ideally the program is suited for both men and women.

"This treatment approach has been successful in other locations. You owe your patients the opportunity to receive more than just custodial care, and you would be giving your staff the chance to be trained in Behavior Modification techniques. The ward you choose can serve as a model for extending Behavior Modification throughout the Institution."

Zeb Ramsey sold himself and his program to Dr. Bahai, who chose Sharon Lovejoy's ward to serve as the guinea pig.

The nurses hadn't heard much about Behavior Modification before, only that it used the method of rewarding good behavior, and punishing bad behavior. At least, that's what they thought it meant. They wouldn't know for sure until the program was implemented, and Zeb Ramsey was going to make sure that would happen.

The first thing this newly-hired staff psychologist did in his new office was to set about writing an application for his grant. Zeb Ramsey saw Dunton as a fertile field, just waiting to be mowed.

"Now let's see," he said, taking pen and paper in hand and starting to write. "If I make this sound complicated enough, the dumb bureaucrats won't understand it. Therefore, they'll think it's so important that it would be a crime not to fork over the money!"

So he began...

> ...for the greater coordination of philosophy and treatment...create a meaningful and positive community... with appropriate behavior repertoire...potential back-up reinforcers...the critical variables controlling ongoing appropriate and inappropriate behaviors, using the techniques outlined above in a contingent environment...

"There!" he thought, holding his paper up like a trophy. "I defy them to understand that!"

When Zeb Ramsey's application was approved, the Institution received a three-hundred-thousand-dollar grant to put his program into effect. Sharon Lovejoy was asked to prepare for the redistribution of patients, both male and female, to and from her ward, to participate in the Behavior Modification program.

"I'm almost at the end of my rope," she told Laurie one evening at supper time in the employees' dining room.

"What's been going on?" Laurie asked.

"I wonder if I didn't make a big mistake," answered Sharon, "agreeing to work on the male violent ward. It's such a dingy, dirty place. The mattresses are lumpy and stained with urine; there's nothing for the patients to do, and they get locked in seclusion rooms for the most minor infractions. When I first got there, I counted over fifty percent of the men zonked -- sleeping on benches or on the floor."

"I remember," Laurie said. "I saw them during my orientation."

"Well, the pharmacy attendant had reported an excessive amount of drugs being ordered for that ward. I checked the amount ordered from the pharmacy against that ordered by the doctors, and found that it was double! So the attendants have just been zonking the patients to make their work easier."

"It sounds as though you've got your work cut out for you, Sharon, but I know you're up to the challenge," Laurie said, trying to be encouraging.

"I really haven't done much yet," Sharon said. " I sewed a few curtains and cut some pictures out of some old calendars to put up on the wall. Now, *I'm* the only one ordering the medication, so the patients are becoming a lot more alert."

"I'm glad they've got someone up there looking out for them," Laurie said. "What they need is a little compassion, and to know that someone cares."

"You should have seen their faces, Laurie, when I threw a big birthday party for all of them yesterday."

"How did you manage that?" Laurie asked.

"I bought four cake mixes, and borrowed a large cake tin from the Recreation Department. They were like kids at Christmas time when they saw me walk in with that huge cake."

"It sounds to me as though you're getting along really well," declared Laurie.

"And now they're asking me to take on a Behavior Modification program, for God's sake, and I don't even know what it means. I would like to modify some of these doctors' behaviors, though," complained Sharon.

"What do you mean?" asked Laurie.

"Dr. Mezummi is getting worse lately, about teasing the patients. The last time he 'tripped' the ward, he went up to John Dexter, who's highly disturbed to begin with, and said, 'I heard that Miss Stanley crawled in your bed last night.' John called him a damned liar, taking him very seriously, of course, but Mezummi shot right back with, 'She told me you have an awful good wang, but she's mad at you, because you didn't stay with her long enough'."

"How dare he say such things to a patient?" Laurie responded, indignantly. "It would have served him right if John had smashed him."

"He almost did," said Sharon. "He started lunging toward him, shaking his fists and practically foaming at the mouth. And do you know what Mezummi did? He ran behind me, and just stood there. I told him I thought he was a real coward, hiding behind a woman's skirt. Anyway, we had to call an attendant to subdue John."

"And as if that weren't enough, he started riling Eben Gates. Right in front of him, he said to me, 'Do you see this patient here? He raped a ten-year-old girl. Do you still think he's worthy of your devoted care and attention?'"

"Eben started ranting and raving and never let up until long after Mezummi had left the ward."

"Such indignities that people suffer," said Laurie, sadly, "when they are left with no choices in their lives."

"But speaking of suffering, that really isn't the worst of it, Laurie."

Sharon went on to describe the painful procedures done on the ward, without benefit of anesthesia, such as the removing of injured toenails, or the incising and draining of wounds.

"I'm sorry to have 'dumped' on you like this, Laurie," Sharon said, "but I needed to confide in someone to keep from blowing my top."

"You won't blow your top," Laurie assured her. "It's just being in this place, and seeing all this injustice."

"Effie Dawson was transferred out of Doris Pitts's ward today to the 'bed- side'," Laurie said, disgustedly, "just because she's had to have a retention catheter which needs daily irrigations. Effie's not a 'bed-side' patient, but no patient is allowed on Doris Pitts's ward unless she can do everything for herself. And now I'm afraid that Effie will go right down hill, being around all those bed patients with no one to talk with. That's what I call an injustice."

Returning to the Annex after her supper break, Laurie 'tripped' A-6 first, wondering if Perley's new order for Valium was helping him. He seemed to be resting comfortably, and all else was fine on the ward.

A patient walked up to her and said, "I think you're a rotten son of a bitch, and I'd like to kick you in the ass."

He took a few steps away from her, turned back again and said, "Erase that."

"Okay, Louie," Laurie said. She was used to his comments by now. He always said whatever was on his mind, and then, without fail, followed up his sometimes outrageous monologues with the statement, "Erase that," figuratively wiping the slate clean and making everything okay again.

Going downstairs to A-3, another patient stopped her to confide the fact that she had seen the aide going into the elevator and staying there a long time, with Dr. Mezummi.

"When could she possibly do this?" Laurie asked. She couldn't simply take the patient's word for such as accusation; after all, these patients often had delusions, seeing things and hearing voices that weren't real.

But the patient said, "She does it after the supervisor comes around for the last time in the evening."

"All right, I'll make a note of it," Laurie said, filing this bit of information in the back of her mind. Of course, as she reasoned, "I wouldn't put it past that oily Mezummi, but I'll need more proof than mere hearsay!"

She worked her way up through the wards, and on A-ll, she happened to look out the window with its view onto the courtyard, and saw a light flashing from an A-3 window below.

"What's that?" she asked one of the aides.

"That's Crowley signaling her boyfriend, Mezummi," the young woman said.

"What are you talking about?"

"She signals him every night, and he goes to the ward."

It was that simple and it was true.

"Well, I'd better do something about that," Laurie said, going down to A-3 and almost bumping into Dr. Mezummi.

"What are you doing here?" she asked. "You're not on duty."

"Oh, I just thought I'd drop in to see how things were going," he said. Then he pushed her against the wall, pressing himself against her.

"Cut it out," she yelled, struggling from his grip, as Crowley came down to see what the commotion was. She gave the doctor a wink, as if it were all a big joke, but Laurie was angry enough to say, "I'll report you if I ever find out that you've left these patients unattended!"

That same night, the security guard found Crowley and Mezummi in the 'grove', where patients with ground privileges sometimes went for a roll in the hay. After he reported the incident, the aide was fired, but Dr. Mezummi's punishment consisted only of being called on the carpet and being made to say he was sorry, like a little boy who had done some mischief in grammar school, and had to stand in a corner.

Harrowing stories about the Behavior Modification program were circulating throughout the wards. In theory, the plan was to teach patients to become self-reliant by compelling them to be responsible. They were given tokens in payment for performing their tasks or exhibiting socially-acceptable behaviors. The tokens were necessary in order to purchase anything they needed, including meals and bed. If a patient didn't have the necessary tokens, then he would have to forfeit a meal.

But if they didn't do their assigned tasks, such as washing the dishes, or mopping the floor, and weren't given any tokens, they were also punished by being made to stand in corners or sit with their heads on tables, and Sharon began to notice that some of them were losing weight, since they weren't eating.

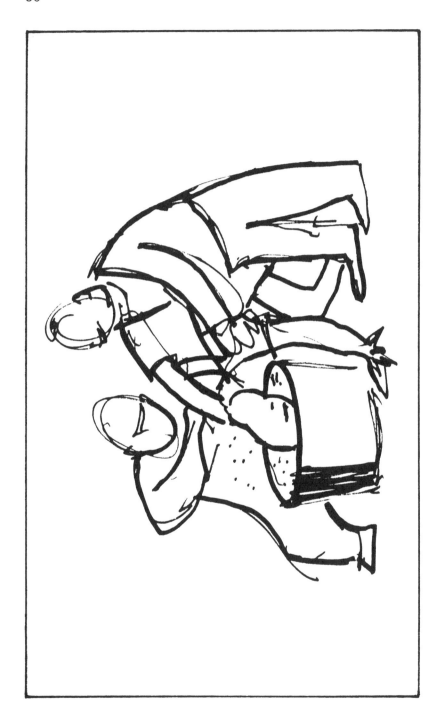

"How far are they going to let this go?" she thought, as she saw an incontinent patient being asked to wash up the puddle she had made on the floor. The patient stared vacantly at the attendant with the mop in his hands, not able to comprehend what she was expected to do.

Suddenly Sharon saw the attendant and a female aide whom he had called to his side, pick up the patient, turn her upside down, and put her head in the pail of water.

Sharon started screaming and running toward them to put a stop to this incredible, savage cruelty.

"What the hell do you think you're doing?" she yelled, and the attendant had the nerve to answer, "We're just trying to motivate this patient."

When they returned her to a standing position, water running down her face mixing with her tears, Sharon said, "You're on report, both of you. You can leave this ward immediately!"

Sharon called Zeb Ramsey to the ward and told him what had happened. Strangely enough, it hardly seemed to affect him.

"You know," he said, "we're trying to teach these patients some responsibility, but you nurses are too indoctrinated in your own philosophy which tends to be dependency-creating."

"Dependency creating?" Sharon said, fighting to keep her voice and her anger down. "We're here to help the patients because they can't help themselves."

"But don't you see?" he replied. "They can never learn to help themselves if you do everything for them! Don't you see that it's a vicious circle?"

Sharon reported everything that happened to Grace Maybury, who said, "I'll pass this on to Dr. Bahai, but I can't promise anything. I haven't gotten any support since Dr. Atherton died."

As she had expected, Dr. Bahai was at a complete loss to help them.

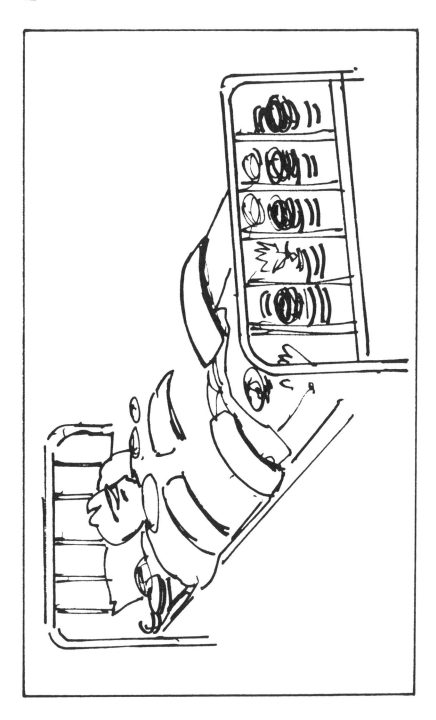

"It's a separate program," he said, "run independently from the rest of the Institution. Our physicians aren't even permitted on that ward unless they are summoned."

"Well, it doesn't seem right," Maybury said, "that they should have complete control of this program, doing whatever they please, with no accountability to anyone."

The following day when Sharon reported for duty and was making rounds with the off-going, eleven-to-seven-shift aide, she saw Freddie Simmons restrained, wrists and ankles tied to his bed. The mattress had been removed and Freddie was lying on the naked bed springs.

"But this is impossible!" she said. "We can't let this happen. Why is Freddie being treated this way?"

"Because he wet his bed last evening," the attendant said. "He refused to change the sheets himself, so Dr. Ramsey told them to take his mattress away and let him sleep on the bare springs. But he wouldn't sleep on the bare springs, so they restrained him, and that's how he had to sleep all night."

"Well, unrestrain him right now," Sharon ordered, "and if you don't do as you're told, I'll have you fired!"

She called Zeb Ramsey right away, and he said to her, "You don't seem to be fitting into this program very well, Miss Lovejoy. That is, you don't seem to understand that this could be a very effective negative reinforcement for eliminating this behavior."

"But it's not working!" Sharon said, "and as far as I'm concerned, what you call 'negative reinforcement' is abuse, pure and simple."

She hung up the phone, shaking her head back and forth in total disbelief. "They could send you away, lock you up in jail, and throw away the key, for all I care!" she mumbled, staring ahead of her, down the middle of the ward, with patients on their beds on either side, and she was staring with the same, blank, uncomprehending look that most of them had in their eyes.

When Zeb Ramsey hung up the phone, he stalked right into Grace Maybury's office and said, "Sharon Lovejoy has not been fitting into our program. She's been hostile and uncooperative ever since its inception. You nurses seem to lack orientation to the psychosocial needs of the patient. I see no hope for a working relationship between us. I want Sharon Lovejoy off my unit!"

CHAPTER EIGHT

Perley Grave's condition seemed to grow worse every day, and Laurie couldn't help but make a connection between his faltering will to live and the decline of the Institution itself.

Dr. Lucas Shada was the next opportunist to appear on the scene, and in the month following his grand entrance, he had already convinced Dr. Bahai of the "necessity" of having a Skilled-Care unit at Dunton, to be funded, naturally, by the State.

When his application was approved, thousands of tax dollars were spent in renovations and the purchase of supplies and equipment such as cardiac monitors, defibrillators, and piped-in oxygen for each room in this basement-unit. And if a few thousand dollars found their way into his pockets, as they most certainly did, then that would profit the Institution too, since he would be happy, which would make him work well, which would then make the program work even better.

Dr. Shada was the first American-trained physician to join the staff after Dr. Atherton's death, and at first he appeared humble and grateful for any assistance or consideration he was given. Despite his minority background, he was given the red-carpet, high-status treatment by Dr. Bahai, who believed his credentials to be superior.

But in a very short while, Dr. Shada began to show his true colors. He canvassed the Institution in search of its best help for his unit. He told them that they would be responsible only to him, banking on this as a giant incentive for transferring into his unit, but which was absolutely false.

But when a flood of requests started pouring into Grace Maybury's office for transfer to Dr. Shada's unit, the Director of Nurses called the doctor in to speak to him personally.

"I am going to have to refuse the bulk of these transfers," she told him. "If I pull all of my best nurses and aides off their regular positions, there won't be anyone capable left to handle the majority of our patients."

"If I were Caucasian," Dr. Shada said, so emotionally charged that the hair seemed to stand up on his skin, "then you would see that my Skilled-Care unit were properly staffed, wouldn't you?"

"What nonsense!" she said. "I've never heard such rubbish. Why, you act as if you already own this Institution. Well, let me tell you something. Caucasian or Filipino, or New Zealander, you will have to learn to work with the staff that I assign to you, or you will have no staff at all! And one thing's for sure -- you will never, never get anywhere without my cooperation. So you'd better watch yourself, Dr. Shada!"

She would show him where the real power at Dunton lay. She would show him a thing or two.

But Grace Maybury would have a lot of trouble on her hands proving herself to be top dog over Dr. Shada. Unfortunately, he was successful at recruiting one of her best nurses, Muriel Avery.

Muriel gave up her position to accept this greater challenge, and worked very hard setting up his Skilled-Care unit, putting in many long work days.

When the unit became operational, largely due to her efforts, Dr. Shada told Muriel that he was bringing in another nurse to be in charge of it, and that her services would no longer be required.

Shocked and dismayed, Muriel went straight to Grace Maybury who was infuriated at the man's audacity.

"Where the hell do you get off doing a thing like that?" she demanded over the phone. "Who the hell do you think you are? You don't have any right to hire or fire nurses!"

He did not respond in kind, but merely said, "Thank you, Mrs. Maybury, for your concern," and hung up the phone.

Grace's complaint to Dr. Bahai met with deaf ears. Dr. Bahai was not about to tangle with Lucas Shada.

Having filled the position that Muriel vacated in order for her to transfer to Dr. Shada's unit, and having no other positions available in the Main Building, Grace sent Muriel to work at the Annex.

Efforts to get sick patients admitted into this new Skilled-Care Unit were meeting with a great deal of resistance. Although the physicians were writing orders for patient transfers, most were being turned down. If patients were not considered curable, they were refused admittance. It would appear that the patients who required the most care couldn't get it from the unit supposedly most qualified to provide it. Although the unit was well-staffed and well-equipped, it remained less than half full.

Shortly after the funding for Dr. Shada's unit was procured, Rick Armstrong, the new head of Recreational Therapy, proposed to Dr. Bahai that he apply for participation of the Annex in the Medicaid program, making the Annex a licensed Extended Care Facility, which would qualify *it* for government funding.

"But the Annex would need an administrator," Dr. Bahai argued. Rick smiled and sat back in his chair, and said, "Yes, and I'm prepared for that too. As a matter of fact, I'm taking an administrator correspondence course right now, so I will be qualified for that position," thinking at the same time that he would also be qualified to get those nurses over there to work their butts off for him, and take all the credit himself.

This position would provide Rick with a substantially higher salary and a boost to higher places.

When Laurie reported for duty that afternoon, she was informed that Lula Bagley would be moving over to the Main Building.

"All hell's breakin' loose," as Bagley put it, briefing Laurie. "I might as well tell you now that you're gonna have an administrator over here, and I'm goin' over to the Main Buildin' to be Mrs. Maybury's assistant. Sharon Lovejoy and Muriel Avery will be comin' over here."

"Why is that?" asked Laurie.

"They've been kicked off their own units in the Main Buildin', and since all supervisors over here have to be licensed nurses on account of the new regulations, they'll be comin' over."

Bagley went on to explain, "The Annex is goin' under title nineteen, which means it's gonna be a Medicaid facility. Rick Armstrong from Recreational Therapy is gonna be your new boss. I don't know what you're gonna do with Hoxie."

It was a little after eight P.M. Laurie had finished making second rounds and had locked all the doors to the outside, when she was paged to go to A-6. Perley Graves was having an acute anxiety attack. His breathing was shallow and rapid.

Since she knew he was hyperventilating, she asked him to take some slow, deep breaths.

"Now just relax," she said to him. "I'm going to call the doctor and get an order for some new medicine to help calm you down."

Since he was already on Valium, Dr. Gallino, the doctor on call, ordered Thorazine 50 mgm. to be given as necessary for anxiety. Laurie administered the medication and sat with him until he had settled down.

"He's wasting away," she thought, "and it's no wonder. He's just lost the will to live."

New Annex administrator, Rick Armstrong, called his nurses together for a meeting.

After introducing himself, he outlined what he explained as his preferred method of treatment.

"Milieu Therapy is a system whereby the environment is set up to give residents the opportunity to assume the normal roles we find in society. And by the way, you noted that I referred to our patients as residents.

"I think that's a welcomed change," agreed Sharon.

Rick went on to explain. "For instance, I would like you to set up a community store staffed by the residents. If they're allowed to carry some of their own money with them, they can act as store owners or consumers."

"I would also like you to arrange sitting areas on the wards, so the residents can get together and socialize. I know that may sound radical, but it there's no place for the residents to sit together, they will never learn to become each other's friends."

"It's so simple, really, isn't it? Maybe you could even have parties for them once in a while," he said.

"I don't see why you seem to think that simple, everyday humane treatment of patients is radical, Rick," said Sharon. "We've been trying to do these things for them for a long time, without any special acknowledgment, and have even been yelled at for making changes."

"Well, all of that is going to change now," Rick said. "You work for me now, and no one else."

Rick then drew their attention to a large chart on which he had outlined his proposed changes in the Annex organizational structure.

"As you see on this chart, there is no more 'up-side' or 'bed-side', but rather Psychiatric Unit A and Medical Unit B.

"I want to bring you, Laurie, onto the day shift, to become the Unit A Chief as soon as we can hire someone else to fill your three-to-eleven-supervisor slot."

"You, Muriel, will be more suitable as the Medical Unit B Chief, since you are not very comfortable with the new programs, and we'll be instituting Milieu Therapy on Unit A."

Muriel nodded in agreement.

"What will become of me?" Sharon asked jokingly.

"Your new title, Sharon, will be Annex Director of Nursing."

"How big a raise comes with our impressive new titles?" asked Sharon.

Rick laughed embarrassingly and continued. "My main objective as administrator of this facility is to improve the quality of life for our patients. I believe that the best way of accomplishing this will be for all of us to work together as a team in order to develop a plan of care for each."

"Who would this team consist of?" asked Muriel.

"Everyone who has to do with the care of the patients," he answered, "including the Social Worker, the Psychologist, the Occupational Therapist, the Physiotherapist, the Activity Director, the Unit Chief, and last but not least, the Team Leader."

"Who would that be?" asked Sharon.

"The aide in charge of each ward will now be referred to as the 'Team Leader'," he explained, "and it will be her responsibility to request the team meetings."

"I assume that it will then be the responsibility of the Unit Chief to coordinate these meetings," stated Laurie.

" That is correct," he said. "In order to comply with the new Medicaid requirements, all the patients' records will be brought onto the wards."

"That will be a switch," Laurie said. "They were always kept off the wards in accordance with Dr. Atherton's strict orders."

"He was always afraid that the intimate and private nature of the patients' histories might turn into blackmail fodder for any meddling and unscrupulous staff," Sharon added.

"Well," replied Rick, "that which has been forbidden is now mandated."

"It will be good to know something about our patients," said Laurie. " It will certainly aide us in developing their care plans. I'm glad the exception has turned into the rule."

"Can you give us some examples of what these care plans would consist of," asked Muriel, "and when it would be appropriate for a team leader to request a team meeting?"

Rick reiterated, "It is my main objective to improve the quality of life for our patients. For instance, if a team leader on the 'bed-side' had a patient whom she felt was socially aware, it would then be appropriate for her to request a meeting of the treatment team to discuss the possibility of that patient being transferred to the 'up-side' where he or she would have the opportunity to socialize."

"That patient would then have the opportunity to participate in the Milieu Therapy program which will be implemented on the 'up- side', or Psychiatric Unit A," added Laurie.

"That is a good case in point," said Rick. "And another appropriate reason for requesting a treatment-team meeting would be to discuss, and hopefully resolve any problems -- medical, behavioral, or any others -- which may occur."

"I do want to make one thing very clear," Rick declared, "I don't want any handicapping condition to keep a socially-aware patient off Unit A."

"Does that include being confined to a wheelchair?" Laurie asked.

"Yes," he answered, "That includes being confined to a wheelchair."

"What if a patient requires a treatment?" asked Laurie, thinking of Effie Dawson who got shunted off to a bed ward because she had a catheter which needed daily irrigations.

"We won't be holdin' a patient back on a bed ward, which we'll now call Unit B, because some staff person on Unit A doesn't wanna do a treatment," answered Rick, sharply.

"I'm very relieved to hear that," she responded.

"I want you to write your own job descriptions of what you do," continued Rick, "and by the way, what does Mathilda Hoxie do around here anyway? No one seems to know. You'd better write up a job description for her too. We should use her somehow, if she's going to be paid."

"That might be a little difficult," said Sharon. "She hasn't done any actual work for so long."

"Okay now," said Rick, "let's get on our way to reorganizing the Annex from a custodial to a treatment-oriented facility!"

The Annex staff rejoiced, as the old regime came to an end, without imagining the tyranny that was to follow.

CHAPTER NINE

A new superintendent had been hired. His name was Hal Zacharias. After his first staff meeting, it was the general consensus of opinion that he must have been a prison warden in his prior job.

He opened his first meeting by dropping a bombshell.

"My main commitment at Dunton will be to reduce the burden of this State's taxpayers by appreciably lowering the patient population."

"What percentage of patients would you people say actually need to be here?"

Although there were almost fifty staff members present in the conference room, no one dared to answer his question, since they were all shocked by the revelation that his main purpose as an administrator would be to reduce the patient -- and therefore the staff -- population as much as possible.

"Well, since you all seem too afraid to respond, let me continue by saying that we will not only reduce the current population, but will also be revamping our admissions policy, admitting only the mentally ill and not the physically disabled or elderly. Senility is a normal step in the aging process, and this is not a nursing home, and this State can no longer be responsible for the care and feeding of everyone's unwanted 'dotty' old great-aunts.

"This Institution is not a dumping ground, so you'd better be prepared for closing down up to half of the wards, so that we here at Dunton will be caring for only those patients who actually fit the appropriate placement descriptions, as outlined in my new policies."

Although Laurie and Sharon were both bursting with questions about the new goals for the Institution and for the patients, their tongues were tied when it came time in Hal Zacharias's meeting to ask any questions they might have, or to offer any suggestions.

As Laurie 'tripped' her wards following that decisive staff meeting, she became sadly aware that it was not only the employees who feared being terminated. She noticed on A-3 that Ina Brooks was wearing her underwear over her dress.

"What's going on with her?" she asked aide Barbara Garson.

Oh, word's been leaking out that the new Superintendent wants to ship out a lot of the patients. Ina thinks that if she acts crazy enough, she'll be allowed to stay. Some of the others are being incontinent for the same reason."

"How pitiful," Laurie said, "that these poor souls now have to worry about where they'll be spending the rest of their lives. I don't think the ones who've been here a long time will make it. It'll just be too traumatic for them."

"If they close half of the wards, they certainly won't be able to use all of us around here anymore," said Garson, worriedly. "And to think I wanted to work here because of the job security."

"Well, I certainly hope we don't lose you, Garson," Laurie said, "and I hope they don't choose to let me go either!"

Laurie hadn't given much thought to the possibility of the end of her career at Dunton. As she approached A-6 to see Perley that night, she realized that the administration was probably justified in wanting to get rid of some dead weight, but it was frightening to imagine that in pruning the Dunton tree, they might also be cutting off a limb with her name on it.

Perley's body was now emaciated, and it was becoming almost impossible for him to tolerate being out of bed.

"He's just wasting away," Laurie thought, trying to hide her pity at seeing him. And he was shaking very badly, which was a common side effect of the medication he was on. But the symptoms were irreversible, and Laurie wondered if the cure wasn't worse than the disease

"I've just got to do something for him," she thought. She decided to call the duty doctor right away, and ask for permission to transfer Perley to Dr. Shada's new Skilled-Care unit.

"Sure," replied Dr. Bauer. "Go ahead and make the arrangements, and I will write the order later."

But when Laurie made the request, the nurse at the other end of the phone asked, "What is his potential for improvement?"

"Not good," Laurie answered, "but he needs a lot more care than we are able to give him over here."

"I'm sorry," the nurse said. "He does not meet the criteria for admission to this unit."

So Laurie helped to move him to A-ll, on Unit B, and couldn't help thinking that there was no room at the Inn for this poor man.

"Leave him alone; he's better off dead!" Louie whispered in her ear. He had shuffled up behind her without her noticing his presence, since she had been daydreaming.

"Better off dead?" she said, turning around to give him a cold stare.

"Erase that," he said, his head lowered down onto his chest.

"What are you doing over here anyway?" she asked him, getting up to walk him back to his ward. He must have wandered off when no one was looking, and Lord knows where he might have ended up if she hadn't been there

"Why do they pace back and forth, some of them?" Laurie wondered, returning the errant patient back where he belonged.

"Why do they sit and rock for hours, sucking their thumbs or pulling on the same strand of hair, curling it around the same finger over and over again?"

She stood very still, simply watching the scene unfold itself around her. Some were catatonic, unmoving, their eyes unblinking, locked into the terror in their minds' eyes, while others shivered and trembled, shaking unceasingly, moving constantly but going nowhere, like laundry hanging on a line blowing nowhere in the wind.

"If only someone would talk to them!" she thought, knowing that no amount of progressive new programs would be of any help to these 'residents', if no one followed through by talking to them. But when they were simply...dumped, as Hal Zacharias said; when they were simply dumped into institutions, then how could anyone expect them to improve?

"This *is* a dumping ground," she thought.

In a very short while, Hal Zacharias called his second staff meeting.

"I have been negotiating," he explained, "with certain nursing homes in the area, for the transfer of some of our patients. Of course, they won't get as much money from the State as they get for their private patients, but they'd rather fill their beds, and take what they can get."

"Where is the savings for the taxpayers there?" said Laurie to Sharon who was sitting next to her.

"Yeah, that just sounds like it's going out of one pocket and into the other!" Sharon said, as Hal Zacharias continued.

"The 'parlor' wards have top phase-out priority, of course. I know those patients are all in a dither over the prospects of leaving, but they're gonna have to learn that this ain't no hotel. If they can sit around all day, smokin' cigarettes, watchin' television and makin' coffee for themselves, plus go out on leave every weekend, then they can just go out and stay out!"

"And I've noticed that you nurses are making this relocation process difficult by trying to hang onto the patients. You've got to change your attitudes. You like to keep them dependent on you. It's a big ego-trip for you. What do you want? -- to keep them living forever?"

Grace Maybury stared at him, her face beet red. But she was speechless. So was the rest of the group -- at his callousness -- and fearing for the security they had worked so long to attain.

Many would be losing their jobs, as Hal Zacharias's plans included clearing out the 'good' patients, and redistributing the others, in order to phase out half of the wards, as well as the remaining, unnecessary positions. A-1, Doris Pitts's self-care ward, was designated as the first to go, causing great anxiety for Grace Maybury, who would have difficulty finding another such position for Pitts.

"You can have A-3, Barbara Garson's ward," Grace Maybury promised. "Those patients are not very difficult. I'll move Garson to the 'bed-side'."

"What about Sharon and Rick?" Doris asked.

"Sharon has been planning her vacation for next week. I'll take care of it while she's gone."

"Well you just better do something," Doris warned, "that is if you know what's good for you. I don't intend leaving this place without my pension, and I don't intend working on a 'shit' ward either."

When Sharon returned from her vacation, she was infuriated to see what had transpired during her absence. She complained to Rick Armstrong, who in turn called Grace Maybury.

"I'm the boss over here," he said, "and I don't want you moving my staff around."

"I'm still the boss, buddy," Grace yelled back at him, "and I'll reassign my staff as I choose, and don't you ever forget it!"

As the weeks wore on, news trickled back to Dunton that many of the discharged patients were dying from the shock of relocation, or from neglect. Nothing could be done about it, and it was a period of grief that made Laurie think of what it must be like to live through a lethal epidemic.

Some of the patients were living through the ordeal, but without being able to manage it too successfully.

Flossie Higgins had been a patient at Dunton for twenty-five years, ever since she was ten years old, and tried to burn her house down. She simply didn't know what to do with her new-found freedom.

Before her release, Flossie had unearthed some background information on some of the staff, including where they lived. She could not understand why they would not welcome her into their homes when she knocked on their doors, and at times would become so nasty and belligerent that the police had to be called to remove her.

One evening, Flossie decided she would have a night on the town. She made her way to a local cocktail lounge, and after having a few drinks, which didn't mix well at all with her tranquilizers, she got up and started waltzing around the dance floor -- not very gracefully in her heavy Oxfords -- dressed in an old-fashioned dress and shawl, issued to her from Dunton's donated-clothing room. She stopped now and then at a table to make a romantic gesture to some of the male customers, making quite a spectacle of herself.

Thrilled with being the center of attention, she got carried away and started doing a strip-tease. But then of course, her dream came to an end when the police were called. Flossie was on the heavy-set side, and strong as an ox when riled. It took four policemen to finally subdue her. This time, she was taken straight back to Dunton. The police had had their fill of Flossie, and that was the end of her freedom.

As Unit-A Chief, Laurie worked with her staff in setting up formats for their wards which reflected the new treatment focus. There were actually some positive changes taking place. The patients were now scheduled to attend the Activity Area -- converted from the basement bed ward -- for sewing, knitting and other craft projects. They were taken on shopping trips to buy attractive clothing, which renewed their interest in their own appearances. They were encouraged to help care for their own clothes, to make their own beds, to bake cakes and have bake sales, and to take turns working in the patient-run store

To allow for socialization, sitting-room areas needed to be set up on the wards. One afternoon, Rick Armstrong asked Laurie to go with him to the recently-vacated Nurses' Residence to choose some appropriate furniture for that purpose. Hal Zacharias had earlier evicted all the live-in personnel, advising them that the Institution would no longer be providing them with cheap room and board. Rick had decided to take it upon himself to requisition some of this idle furniture for use in his program.

"Do we have the right to just help ourselves to whatever we feel like taking from this building?" Laurie asked Rick. "Can we get into trouble with Zacharias?"

"No," answered Rick. "He can't get rid of me. I'm the only licensed administrator he's got. I'm the only one he respects around here, and do you know why?"

"Why?" asked Laurie.

"Because I'm the only one who's got the guts to tell him he can take his goddam job and stick it up his butt!"

She wondered, of course, if Rick would ever have said as much to Hal Zacharias, himself. At any rate, the requisitioned furniture did not remain on the wards for long.

The Unit-A staff, with the exception of Doris Pitts, embraced the new program, eager to give more meaning to their patients' lives. The status quo, however, was doing just fine for Doris, and she was not about to allow any new administrator or supervisor to disrupt it.

CHAPTER TEN

It was on a Sunday that Perley died. Laurie had tried again to get him admitted to Dr. Shada's Skilled-Care unit, but was told again that if he was terminal, he did not meet the criteria for admission. Laurie documented this in a special record book that Grace Maybury had ordered all the units to keep of patients refused admission to that new facility.

Perley's skin had taken on a gray-yellow tinge, and even with his feeding tube in, he had vomited constantly and had needed much more attention than the Annex staff was able to provide.

Laurie had arranged to have his bed moved into a small, empty room, so that he could at least die in peace and privacy. His voice was so weak by then that she could hardly hear him, but he was still tormented by his morbid delusion, and he kept crying out that he was never going to die, just fall forever into a bottomless pit.

"There is no bottomless pit," Laurie said to him, wondering if he was past the point of understanding her, but trying nonetheless to ease his suffering.

"You won't just keep falling forever, Perley, because it doesn't work that way. There's really nothing to be afraid of. Do you understand me?"

She had the feeling she was speaking to someone fast asleep, but that didn't stop her from trying.

She phoned the doctor on call to see if he could make Perley's last moments any easier. Dr. Roy Black was an American-trained physician, fairly new to the Institution. He had gotten through medical school by the skin of his teeth, and had failed to pass board exams.

"Let me know when he expires," Dr. Black said, "and then I'll come over and 'pronounce' him."

"But he needs help," Laurie explained. "His breathing is labored and he's very apprehensive. I think you'd better come and see him."

"Oh, all right," the doctor said, slamming down the phone, obviously distraught at the untimely interruption of his weekend at home.

When he arrived, he examined Perley, shrugged his shoulders and said, "You're right. I don't think he'll last much longer. I guess I'll just hang around until it's over. No sense in making two trips. Say, do you have a newspaper? I'll just sit in the chart room until he's gone."

Laurie was seething mad as she walked out of Perley's room, and as soon as they were out of earshot, she turned on her heel and said, "How could you talk that way in front of a patient? Didn't you learn any professionalism at all? And don't you have any compassion?"

"That man wants to die, for God's sake," the doctor said, picking up a newspaper and rolling it up in his hand, then swinging it back and forth like a baton as he spoke. "And do you think he can understand what's going on? Why, he probably doesn't comprehend anything anymore."

"But he's still a human being," Laurie said, unintimidated by the doctor's cruelty and coldness. "And he deserves to be treated with respect, whether he understands or not."

As the doctor walked away from her, she said to herself, "Don't lose it now; don't lose your temper!"

She went downstairs to the employees' lounge to cool off and splash cold water on her face, and just get away for a while.

When she returned to Perley's ward, Dr. Black had already pronounced him dead, filling out the necessary reports. He notified Perley's brother and obtained permission for an autopsy to be done. The new regulations mandated the performing of as many 'posts' as possible.

Laurie called the local hospital to let them know that she would be sending over Perley's body. Then she called the Fire Department to advise them that she needed to have a body transported for autopsy.

"We can't transport bodies on weekends," said the voice on the other end of the phone. "We're short-staffed on weekends. What would we do if a real emergency came up?"

"But it was my understanding," Laurie began, as the fireman interrupted her.

"We just can't do it. Sorry, Miss."

Laurie then called Rick Armstrong's home, and was told that he was at church. She got the name of the church and called him there, saying it was a medical emergency.

When he finally came to the phone, and Laurie explained what the fireman had told her, he said, "Well, call the garage man on duty and tell him to take the body over in the back of the wagon."

But when the garage man told Laurie that it was illegal to transport a body in the wagon, Laurie called Rick back and was told he was at the communion rail.

"But this is an EMERGENCY!" she yelled, biting her lip to keep from crying.

A moment later, Rick came back on the line, and when he heard the latest development, he yelled, "Why that stupid bastard! What the hell does he think he's pulling?"

"Do you still have the Host in your mouth," Laurie asked, stifling a nervous giggle.

"I just swallowed it!" he said. "Now you listen to me. It is not illegal to transport a corpse in a wagon as long as you lay it down. I'm gonna call him and blast his ass off!"

A few minutes later, the garage man showed up at the courtyard entrance, where Laurie was waiting with Perley's body.

"Thanks for settin' me up!" he yelled at her, helping the attendant get the body into the wagon.

"It wasn't my intention to set you up, but to get this body to its autopsy," Laurie said. "All I'm asking is that you do your job. That's all! God knows I've done mine. So stop complaining and take this body to the hospital!"

He must have felt some shame at having given her so much trouble, because he tipped his hat at her before he left, and Laurie nodded back to him.

Then she was finally able to go home and rest, secure in the knowledge that Perley was finally at peace.

"The monthly mortality conference is now being held in the large conference room in the Main Building," said the voice over the loudspeaker. "All available staff are requested to attend."

Monthly mortality conferences were held to discuss the cases of patients who had recently died. The pathologist who had performed the autopsies would bring the diseased organs in a large jar of preservative solution, in order to discuss any different treatment approaches that might have increased the patients' lifespans.

The pathologist began by saying, "The first case to be discussed is that of Perley Graves. This patient died in liver failure, due to cirrhosis. Many of you are aware that this patient had a long history of anorexia, even prior to admission. The fundamental cause of cirrhosis is nutritional deficiency."

Removing the organ from the large bottle of solution, the pathologist continued. "You can see that this cirrhotic liver differs from the normal liver in its smaller size and its surface, which is covered with little lumps. Cirrhosis is characterized by necrosis involving the liver cells. It has a very protracted course, occasionally proceeding over a period of many years.

"According to this patient's record, gavage was necessary due to anorexia. As noted, his color became poor, he was nauseated, and had a marked weight loss. I'm surprised, in fact, that this patient was never treated in your new Skilled-Care unit, or sent to the hospital. Can anyone give me an explanation? He must have been in poor condition for weeks, probably months!"

"We never received any request to have this patient admitted to our unit," said Linda Maddox. Linda Maddox was Dr. Shada's hand-picked charge nurse for whom he had dismissed Muriel Avery.

"I beg your pardon," Grace Maybury said, "but I have documentation that states the contrary! In fact, on two separate occasions this patient was refused admission to the Skilled-Care unit. I also have a documented list of other patients who have been refused admission."

The pathologist went on. "A diet high in protein, and liver and Bl2 therapy might have altered the course of his disease. And he was tube-fed for such a long period of time that the procedure irritated the lining of his stomach to an alarming degree."

Hal Zacharias had heard enough. Storming out of the conference room, his long arms swinging at his sides, he stomped down to Dr. Shada's unit, and found him having coffee in the unit's kitchen with some of his staff.

"What's the big idea," he demanded, "of all these empty beds? And where the hell do you get off refusing to take sick patients?"

Shada was visibly shaken. His hair seemed to bristle, but before he even had a chance to respond, Zacharias said, "And you can forget your discrimination crap, you bastard! This Institution has been damn good to you since you arrived. And let me tell you one more thing. If you don't have this unit filled to capacity in one month's time, I'm shuttin' it down!"

Without further ado, Zacharias stormed out of the unit, as Dr. Shada and his staff stared in stunned silence after him.

A few days later, the Superintendent's office circulated a memo from the great man himself. It read, "The Skilled-Care unit has altered its philosophy on admissions. Requests for patient admissions will now be welcomed. Any complaints from this day forward should be addressed to my office, where I will handle each personally."

On the days that followed, Dr. Shada and his nurse, Linda Maddox, could be seen combing the Institution in search of suitable patients to fill the vacancies on their unit.

Shortly after the episode at the Mortality Conference, Laurie ran into Dr. Bahai on A-3. She hadn't seen him in weeks. Since Hal Zacharias had taken over, it was generally assumed that Dr. Bahai was working as the Assistant Superintendent, as he had done for almost twenty years under Dr. Atherton. But that assumption had been incorrect. As it turned out, Zacharias had frozen him right out, not consulting him about anything, and now had re-assigned him to work as a regular staff physician at the Annex. It was shocking for a man who had held such a high-status position for so many years to be demoted so publicly. The staff hoped that it wouldn't be too degrading for him.

When she saw Dr. Bahai, Laurie's heart went out to this man who looked confused and broken.

"You girls are going to have to help me," he said, in a pathetic voice. "It's been a long time since I practiced clinical medicine, and quite frankly, I'm a bit anxious about performing up to par."

"Well, you can count on us," Laurie said to him. "We're really very happy that you've come to join us. Please don't worry. We'll do everything we can to help you."

She felt almost as if she were speaking to one of the patients, trying to console him, but she could tell that her comments didn't change the look of despair in his eyes. He looked very shaken, and said that he was feeling dizzy.

Suddenly, he dropped right where he stood.

"Call the ambulance and Dr. Bauer, and then bring me a pillow," Laurie instructed Pitts.

She put the pillow under Dr. Bahai's head. All of his limbs were limp, and his breathing was slow and deep.

"His pupils are non-reactive," Dr. Bauer said, kneeling down and examining the patient on the floor. "And he has a positive Babinski. It looks as though he's had a CVA."

Dr. Bahai lived only twenty-four hours after his stroke. All available staff from the Institution attended his funeral, and it was a very large gathering. The nurses wore their caps as a sign of their great respect for him.

"I didn't even know him," Sharon said to Laurie, who was standing right next to her. "I only saw him now and then, back in Dr. Atherton's time, when everything was so different."

"I guess he didn't fit into the new scheme of things," Laurie said. "He was like a brave old horse who'd served his master well for years, and then when cars and trucks and planes came to take his place, he wasn't needed anymore."

"You make it sound as if he chose to die, Laurie," Sharon said.

"Maybe he did," she answered.

Everyone laid Dr. Bahai's death at Zacharias's feet, and he knew it. The staff was no longer intimidated by him. Their contempt now overshadowed their fear. He was becoming ineffective, because no one jumped anymore when he spoke. And whether it was his fault directly or not, Hal Zacharias was now being treated as if he were morally, if not criminally, guilty of another man's death.

CHAPTER ELEVEN

Laurie was beginning to worry about Sharon, because she seemed to be losing her old self-confidence. Laurie tried cheering her up by saying, "You don't have to be crazy to work here, but it helps."

"That's part of the problem, Laurie," Sharon said. "I think I am going crazy and I don't know if it's worth it. It's the paperwork that's getting me down more than anything else."

Muriel Avery, Rick's new chief of Medical Unit B, formerly known as the 'bed-side', was having her own set of problems on her unit. A-9, one of Muriel's wards, had been ordered sexually integrated by Superintendent Zacharias as part of an experiment.

One morning, as Muriel was tripping that ward, the sister of one of the patients came running up to her, grabbed her arm, and in a breathless voice said, "I've never seen anything so disgusting in all my life! Men and women together on the same ward, being exposed without privacy! I'm Annie Hopkins' sister, and she told me that a male patient -- the one sitting over there -- walked right up to her, lying helpless in bed, and put his hand right down the front of her johnny."

"This is a difficult situation for all of us," Muriel said to the woman, "but we're just following the orders of our superintendent who believes that these wards should be sexually integrated, the same as in a general hospital. This is the first ward to try this experiment."

"Well, I don't like my sister being used as a guinea pig in some immoral, unhealthy 'experiment'! In a general hospital, there are separate rooms for men and women, aren't there? Or at least curtains dividing the beds, and doors on the bathrooms, and doors on the stalls? But look over there at those patients getting enemas -- not only without privacy, but in view of someone of the opposite sex. Are you just going to stand there and do nothing about it?"

"But what can I do about it?" Muriel was thinking. "I'm only following orders." There weren't enough portable dividers to provide privacy for all the thirty-five patients on the ward, and there had never been any doors on the bathrooms or the stalls, but Muriel felt helpless about changing those facts.

"I'm just as appalled as you are, Ma'am," she said.

"Well, you haven't heard the end of this yet," Annie's sister said. "I'm going to write a scathing letter to my representative in the legislature."

"I think that would be a good idea, and I wish you luck," Muriel said.

After Annie's sister had left, Muriel went up to Annie and asked her, "Did Elmer put his hand down your johnny?"

"Yes, he did," Annie said, "and I was so mad, I almost said something, but I didn't."

Muriel was dreading having to report this incident to newly-hired three-to-eleven supervisor, Faith Byrd, RN, who was always finding some reason to attack her. Faith had been hired to fill that position vacated by Laurie when she transferred to day duty as Unit A Chief. Hired with Faith, as an aide, was her close friend, Rene Boutelle.

In her mid-thirties, Faith was a large woman with a square, shapeless build. Somewhat overweight, she had a small bust, large belly, and broad but flat hips. She was often seen chomping on carrot or celery sticks in an effort to control her appetite, and Muriel thought that Faith took out her aggressions on carrot sticks, biting down on them the way she sometimes bit down on the aides, as if she wanted to bite their heads off.

It was time for the shift report, and Muriel was wondering what Faith would be criticizing her for that day. Muriel was afraid of this mannish woman with her square jaw and piercing blue eyes that sometimes had an evil cast to them. And Faith was so changeable -- a woman of many voices and expressions, her voice ranging from soft and sweet to loud and abrupt, her temperament ranging from demure and beseeching to hostile and threatening. She was a militant women's 'libber', didn't like men very much, and was seriously into the politics of the nursing profession, often lapsing into long tirades about how nurses needed more legislation to protect them under the law.

When Muriel reported the episode with Annie Hopkins, Faith started attacking her for allowing it.

"The order to integrate A-9 came from the Superintendent," said Muriel, in an attempt to defend herself, which she found herself doing more and more where Faith was concerned.

"I don't care who it came from, snapped Faith. "It's deplorable, and I don't think you're much of a nurse, standing still for it."

Muriel, a well-bred, gentle and sensitive woman was left disarmed and trembling by this verbal attack, and was relieved to have this report session interrupted by Linda Maddox, Dr. Shada's charge nurse, who appeared in the doorway and said, "Excuse me, but I've been making rounds on your wards to see if there might be any patients who could benefit from placement on our unit. If you can come up with any recommendations, please feel free to do so."

When she disappeared down the hallway, Faith said, "Well, that's certainly a switch. First we can't get a patient on their precious unit, and now they're begging for them. Well, I'll be damned if I'll help that man fill his unit to keep his ass from getting kicked off this Hill. I heard that Zacharias read him the riot act, and from what I've learned about him, he well deserved it!"

Faith then waved her hand in the air, which meant that Muriel was free to go, and she gratefully left, happy that someone else's problems had come up, taking the burden of her own responsibilities off her shoulders for the moment.

But before leaving, she sat down in the lobby, feeling very inadequate. She needed time to get her wits about her. An excellent nurse, who had forgotten more than Faith would ever know, Muriel was losing what joy she had ever felt in being a nurse. She feared that the odds against her success were too great, and by success, she meant the successful treatment of her patients.

Success, in Faith Byrd's estimation, meant something altogether different. When she and Rene Boutelle had come to Dunton, it was obvious from the first that both of them wanted to end up on top of the pile. They were "going places," as they predicted. Faith would step over the bodies of the men in her path, while Rene would use whichever men she could, not by climbing over them, but by finding her way under them...so to speak.

Rene was a very feminine, attractive girl in her early twenties. Tall, with an exceptionally shapely figure, she was openly seductive, wearing short skirts to show off her lengthy limbs. She kept her long, blonde hair well groomed, and her attitudes were very liberal, especially where sex was concerned. She was completely outspoken about voicing intimate matters, and she would often tell her co-workers which of the men around she wanted to "try out" next.

She made no bones about making a big play for Rick Armstrong, who, old enough to be her father, lapped up her attention and answered her sexual innuendoes with enthusiasm. She referred to him as "Annex's sex object," and they would develop a very close relationship, one that included play as well as work.

As Muriel considered her career, she began to lose confidence in herself, and wondered if she would ever be happy again working at Dunton, now that people like Faith and Rene had come there.

"I'm just tired," she thought, "and I'm not attuned to this new psychosocial kind of treatment either. I guess it's about time I called it a day."

Laurie and Sharon were both saddened to hear the news. Muriel's departure opened up a whole new chapter at the Annex.

Rick Armstrong was in the supervisor's office with Sharon and Laurie, when Faith and Rene reported for evening duty a few days later. They had been consulting on the matter of Muriel's replacement, and had all heartily agreed that Faith was well-suited for the job -- a necessary rung in the ladder to the top.

"I've brought in some activities for the patients to work with," Rene said, rolling her eyes at Rick, who wiggled like a schoolboy. "I'll be bringing them down to the Activity Area later on my break, if anyone would like to come down and look at them!"

She was obviously baiting Rick, and he fell for it, hook, line and sinker. And it was a good excuse to compliment her, since she was only doing what Doris Pitts hadn't been bothered to do. Rene was working as the evening aide on Pitts's ward.

When Faith was offered the position of Chief of Medical Unit B, she said in her *sweet* voice, "I'll try my best to fill Muriel's shoes. You would have to go a long way to find such an excellent nurse as Muriel."

Rick couldn't stop thinking about Rene's offer, or about her long, shapely legs and voluptuous figure. He knew that going downstairs to her would probably lead to trouble. But knowing she was down there, he felt pulled as by a magnet. He couldn't help himself, or stop his heart from racing as he crept down the stairs, across the basement level, toward the Activity Area where she was waiting.

He couldn't stop himself, but he didn't want to stop, so he kept walking, his blood pulsing warmly in his veins.

Then he took a deep breath, went inside, and closed the door.

CHAPTER TWELVE

No one can serve a leader they have no faith in, and a leader loses all of his strength if there is no one left to serve him. So Hal Zacharias got the message, and everyone was overjoyed when he announced his resignation -- especially Dr. Shada, since he felt he had now been given a reprieve, at least for the time being. The Annex staff now made immediate arrangements to put an end to the sexual integration experiment on A-9.

Dr. Nathan Strenge, psychologist, and loyal proponent of Behavior Modification, was next to be named Superintendent of Dunton Mental Institution. One of his first official acts was to eliminate the position of Chief of Psychology, held by Randy Sinclair, demoting him to a staff psychologist and shipping him over to the Annex, which Randy considered equal to being sent to Siberia. Although he hadn't made many friends for himself at Dunton, since he had hardly left his office long enough to get to know anyone, Randy vowed to get revenge on Nathan Strenge, and to defy his every command, the first of which was to "break the back of the nursing stronghold" at Annex.

With Randy now physically out of the way, Dr. Strenge created a new position, Director of Professional Services, to which he appointed Zeb Ramsey. It was Nathan Strenge's goal to extend his program throughout the entire Institution.

Some of the nursing staff laughingly referred to the program as the "BM" program, but Behavior Modification was no laughing matter to Nathan Strenge, who, from his ivory tower, delegated most of his responsibility to his new number-two man, Zeb Ramsey.

To "reinforce" his philosophy throughout the wards, Dr. Strenge hired a team of five psychologist "resource" personnel, whom he named the Program Evaluation and Research Utilization team, commonly referred to as PERU. The function of this team was to devise a new record-keeping system, which was an intricate maze of directions designed to identify problematic behaviors, determine "reinforcers" to be used to modify these behaviors, and set target dates as deadlines for eliminating these behaviors. The irony of this whole matter was that this group would never see a patient, only check the records which were supposed to be developed by the aides on the wards who had neither the background nor the time for such an undertaking.

"It's all a bunch of gobbledygook, if you ask me," Laurie said to Sharon, who was peering down at a mass of papers on her desk, trying to make heads or tails of them.

Suddenly Sharon slammed her fist down on the papers, and said, "It's all so ridiculous, Laurie, that I can hardly believe it. Can you imagine how much time this will take away from the patients. I think they couldn't care less what happens to the human beings in this Institution, as long as their records are properly maintained."

While the two young nurses sympathized with each other, their two older counterparts, Maybury and Bagley, were agonizing over their futures. From the way things were going with Dr. Strenge's plans, Maybury's power was crumbling more and more every day. It was becoming crystal clear that Strenge was out to get her and Bagley once and for all.

They were sitting in Maybury's office, having coffee, when Maybury's secretary handed her a new memo from the Superintendent, headed UNITIZATION PROPOSAL.

Maybury, thinking that that sounded fishy, read it aloud for Bagley to hear.

"The Main Building will be divided into three separate treatment facilities, comprised of three, three, and four wards, respectively. The first will be made up of patients to be discharged to other facilities, the second will become a behavioral unit of 'token economy' wards, and the third will house the long-term residents. Each facility will be headed up by a member of the PERU team, who will have total administrative control over his unit."

"So what does it all mean, Maybury?" asked Bagley.

"It means," Maybury said, rolling the memo into a ball with her fist, "it means they're tryna get me out, but the job's too big for 'em. All they want to do is strut around, lookin' important, shootin' off their big mouths, and collectin' their fat paychecks. My God, I'll bet their salaries are more than two nurses' combined, and they don't even see a patient. They don't give a damn about the patients."

Her eyes grew blank, and she seemed to be staring off into a private place where even Lula Bagley wasn't privileged to enter. But Bagley knew where Maybury had gone, in her mind. She'd gone back to the way the Institution used to be, when Dr. Atherton was still alive. She'd gone back, in her memory, to the glory of the old days, when her power had been absolute, when she and Dr. Atherton had worked so closely together that they were practically like man and wife, like one mind thinking, one heart beating. But the old Dunton wasn't a real place anymore; rather, it was an institution haunted by the long-lost souls of the dead. And nothing that Maybury could do or think of doing or hope for, could ever bring them back again.

And Lula Bagley, watching her in the ghostly silence that had fallen over her face, wondered if Grace would weather this newest storm, and wondered too, just how critical it would be for both of them.

Doris Pitts was still not cooperating to implement Rick's new program, Milieu Therapy.

"The Activity Director has complained again, that she never sees any of your patients in her area," Laurie said, during another confrontation with Pitts.

As Pitts sneered at her, Laurie couldn't help thinking again of Effie Dawson, the patient who had been moved off Pitts's ward because she had to have an indwelling catheter which Pitts didn't want to irrigate.

"You need to pitch in with the rest of us and try to make this program work," said Laurie.

"That would be like trying to get a bunch of trees to start singing and dancing," said Pitts, sarcastically.

"Nevertheless, I want to see some visible evidence soon, that you are making some effort," said Laurie, sharply.

"This is my ward," Pitts answered, defiantly, "and I'll run it the way I choose."

"If you are not interested in participating in this program," Laurie continued, disgustedly, "then perhaps you would be better suited to working on the Medical side."

"If you think you're big enough to make that happen, just go ahead and try," Pitts replied, confidentially.

Laurie was steaming mad. "We'll just see about that," she snapped, stomping out of Pitts's ward.

"This uncooperative employee does not belong on my unit," Laurie told herself angrily, "and I will remove her. To hell with Grace Maybury's order against it."

Although psychologist Randy Sinclair thought it was the biggest waste of his time, he was now forced to attend treatment-team meetings in keeping with the objectives of the new Annex administrator.

A-6 team leader, Louise Corbett, had requested a team meeting, and when she saw him entering the conference room, she said, "Hello, Randy. This is the first time I've seen you out and around."

"That's because this is the first time I've been invited anywhere," he said, slumping down in a chair across the table from her.

"Well, do you need an invitation to make rounds on the wards to see if perhaps some of the patients might avail themselves of your services?" Laurie asked.

"I don't do psychotherapy on patients," Randy said, "because when I do, the staff thinks that they're gettin' preferential treatment and shits on 'em."

"That's an unfair thing to say," Louise said, turning to Laurie as if to ask for her support, "and besides, I don't even think you've been here."

"I don't really care what you think," he said, sarcastically, and then bragged that he had been playing hooky.

"What did Strenge say about that?" Laurie asked, wanting to know if the superintendent was even aware of his absence.

"Apparently, he doesn't know or care what the hell's goin' on. I told him that I just took off for three weeks. And then I asked him, 'Where the hell were you?'"

"What did he say?"

"What the hell could he say? The only thing that bastard could do was keep his trap shut and hope I'd do the same. After all, that wouldn't make him look too good in the eyes of the commissioner. But let's get this stupid meeting started, so we can get it over with. All right?"

Louise Corbett sat up straight and began. "The first patient I'd like to discuss is Rodney Adams. I've tried everything I can think of to get him motivated, and nothing works, so I'm asking for suggestions."

"That's right," echoed Betsy Dunn, the Activity Director. "When he comes down to my area, I can't interest him in anything either. All he wants to do is lie around."

"He gets all upset if I mention his going to a boarding home," Dorothy Sterns, the social worker said, "and boarding homes don't want to take anyone who won't get off his bed."

"Rodney's gettin' on in years now," Randy explained, "and probably realizes he's headin' down the tube. If my guess is right, and I could really say the same thing about a lot of the patients here, he's divorcing himself from his Christless life, and there ain't a damn thing you or anyone else can or should do to motivate him."

"Do you mean we shouldn't even try to interest him in being alive anymore?" Louise said, shocked to hear such a pessimistic attitude.

"Sure. The best thing we could do for him now would be to grease his way down and out. Why don't you ship his ass to the 'bed-side' with the rest of the basket cases?"

Laurie wasn't sure she wanted to hear any more of such outrageous talk.

When Louise began to discuss patient Leroy Lynch who was making sexual demands on another patient on the ward who was retarded and disabled, Randy came up with another shocking recommendation.

"All we need to do is tell Leroy that he shouldn't go around doing what he wants in public, and to wheel his friend into the bathroom, way over to the last stall."

Laurie, as well as most of the others present, was disgusted to hear this statement, and blurted out, "We're not here to find a way for Leroy to continue his behavior! We're here to find a way to eliminate it."

"Why do you want to eliminate it?" Randy asked, leaning back in his chair and chewing on the end of a toothpick. Then he used the toothpick like a pointer, jabbing the air with it as he spoke.

"First of all, how do you know Joey doesn't like it? And second of all, I'm against trying to change anyone's behavior, especially along the lines of those rat psychologists who've moved in and taken over the Institution!"

"Why do you call them rat psychologists?" Dorothy Stern asked.

"Because under their philosophy, people are trained like rats. All of us are sadistic under our tightly controlled social masks. And being given the opportunity to master people brings our sadism right up through the surface, like a fist through a door!"

"Then why should Leroy be allowed to master someone like Joey?" Laurie said. "After all, Joey's unable to speak for himself. He's in a wheelchair for God's sake."

"I fail to see what the problem is," said Rene Boutelle nonchalantly.

Rene had been promoted to Records Consultant, a day position created for her by Rick. She had suggested to him one evening, after the violence of his passion was spent, that she could be of great assistance to the aides on the wards, in writing up their patient treatment-plans now mandated under the new Medicaid regulations. Rick insisted that her new position would qualify her to be a bonafied member of the treatment team.

"I was brought up to believe that whatever anyone wants to do is all right," Rene continued, seductively, "but I do think it should be done privately, as Randy says."

"But that's not the point!" Laurie insisted.

"Don't act like an asshole, Laurie," Randy said, "just because you have hangups."

"I don't have hangups," Laurie said. "If we were talking about two consenting adults, I would have no objection. But we cannot assume that Joey is consenting. He has no means of protecting himself, therefore it is up to us to protect him against Leroy."

"Leroy!" Randy said, laughingly. "Do you know what that means in French? It means, the king! And I guess that's just what Leroy is -- the king of his ward!"

"I'll have to take this up with Rick," Laurie said, "since we can't seem to come to an agreement here."

She was so frustrated suddenly, that she wanted to disappear into the wall like a puff of smoke, and she was hardly listening when the next patient's treatment plan was brought up for discussion. She knew vaguely that it had to do with a man whom Randy said wanted to "disengage" himself from this life.

Laurie caught the tail end of Randy's side of the argument. "...so it would be best just to leave him alone and let him die in peace. But you nurses! You always have to be in control. You can't leave anyone alone -- even when the person has simply given up on life. Sometimes I understand how that could happen, since I'm beginning to feel the same way myself!"

It was beginning to become quite obvious that manipulation was taking place within Laurie's Unit-A treatment team. For some strange and unknown reason, Randy Sinclair was unscrupulously managing to divert any patient requiring care or treatment from Doris Pitts's ward, and on the other hand, retain the self-care patients on her ward. What seemed equally strange was that Rene Boutelle seemed to be collaborating with him in this effort.

While other team leaders in Unit A were accepting medically-impaired, but socially-aware patients into their programs from the 'bed-side' or Medical Unit B, in keeping with the new goals and objectives, Doris Pitts's ward remained unchanged -- a source of much anger and dissension throughout the unit.

When Doris saw patient Lucy Bradley's name on the posted schedule of treatment-team meetings, as a prospective transfer to her ward, she immediately called Randy Sinclair.

"Lucy Bradley is in a wheelchair," she exclaimed ," and can't do anything for herself."

"I know," agreed Randy, "but Rick wants to move the socially-aware patients to the 'up-side' so that they can participate in the program."

"I don't care what Rick wants," Doris exclaimed into the phone. "You'd better do something if you know what's good for you. He's not gonna make a dumpin' ground out of my ward."

Randy was a persuasive talker at that team meeting to discuss Lucy's transfer.

"I feel that there is a risk factor involved in moving Lucy to A-3," he argued. "She would have a serious adjustment problem after being on A-8 for so many years. After all, can anyone here safely predict that she would improve if she were moved?"

"How could anyone safely predict anything like that?" asked A-8 team leader, Martha Linscott.

"And why is it necessary to predict that she'd improve?" said social worker, Dorothy Sterns. "Maybe transferring her to a ward with healthier patients would improve her spirits and help to improve the quality of her life."

"But how would she be improving the quality of her life?" Rene asked.

Randy answered with a question. "Could she go out anywhere -- shopping, lunch, bowling, or even the Activity Area -- in a wheelchair? Who could take her down there every day?"

Even Activity Director, Betsy Dunn was beginning to agree with him. "That's a point," she said. "Even the ambulatory patients on A-3 don't get down to the Activity Area."

"This is going too far," Laurie thought. "Everything seems to be going sour. Whatever is happening to the new goals to improve the quality of life for our patients?"

A critical state of affairs was arising. Laurie's unit was splitting into two camps -- the small but influential group, undermining the program, and the remaining staff who were trying to implement it.

Psychiatric Unit A, formerly the 'up-side', was like a simmering pot, which would soon be boiling over.

CHAPTER THIRTEEN

"What are you laughing at now?" A-5 team leader, Ramona Potter, asked Rene Boutelle.

"I'm laughing at the way you wrote up this treatment plan," Rene said, "and look at the way you spelled technique! It's really laughable, really childish! Boy, it sure is easy to tell the educational level of you people. I don't even see any evidence on this chart that your so-called plan is being carried out. I don't see any sign of any progress notes either. I mean, Rick would just laugh if he saw this record!"

"I hardly have time to write up all these plans, let alone carry them out and then write that up too," Ramona said, "with all the other work I have to do. Besides, I thought that was what you were here for."

"Well, I'm not going to write up these reports for you." Rene said. "I'm a consultant."

Since Rick had created for her the title of Records Consultant, changing her schedule to days, Rene ended up mostly insulting the team leaders, rather than assisting them, causing the morale on Laurie's unit to sink even lower.

"What gives Rene Boutelle the right to come around and make fun of us?" Ramona began, confronting Laurie as she arrived to make rounds on her ward. "What are her credentials anyway? She talks about people with 'low educational levels', but I'll bet she never made it past the sixth grade! Rick should have posted that job he created for her. Maybe some of the rest of us with more seniority would have been interested in taking it, and be more qualified to do it! What did she have to do to get this favor, anyway? Maybe if we knew what it was, we could do it too. Don't you think that would be fun?"

"I don't have the answers, Ramona," Laurie said, "but I'll certainly try to do something about it."

Laurie was getting so many complaints about Rene's belittling remarks and condescending manner, that she decided it was time to have a serious talk with Rick.

Sharon was just tired, that's all. No, in point of fact, she was sick and tired, her head spinning from the talk she'd just had with Faith Byrd, or the talk that Faith had given to her. Faith, as the new Medical Unit-B Chief had started out by asking Sharon a question that was reasonable enough, but she'd ended up lecturing Sharon, who was still trying to adjust to being the Annex Director of Nursing.

"It's about this memo from Dr. Shada," Faith said, barging into Sharon's office with a feminist magazine in one hand and the memo in the other. As she sat down, she said, "Dr. Shada is recommending that nursing personnel be delegated the responsibility of granting or canceling ground privileges for the patients. But doesn't he realize that if anything happens, we'd be the ones held responsible? Do we have any protection under the law? I think not. And I think it's your responsibility to challenge this directive!"

She was speaking, as she often did, in her *dictatorial* voice, her eyes piercing into Sharon's like knives bared for a duel.

"I'll look into it as soon as I can," Sharon said, feeling abused somehow and bruised, as if the other woman were attacking her physically as well as emotionally. She was hoping that Faith would leave right away, but this was only the beginning of Faith's long list of complaints.

"Also, I think we unit chiefs should have the option of interviewing new staff for our units. Why do you let Maybury keep the best people, and palm off the crap and Main-Building rejects on us?"

"I think I can handle the interviewing and hiring of staff, Faith," Sharon declared. "Please don't tell me how to do my job."

"I wouldn't think of it?" Faith said. "But I'm only making some suggestions, or observations! For instance, I think it would be nice to have more supervisors' meetings, so that you can communicate more with your staff. The other shift supervisors don't know what's going on here, and we should all have a job description clearly defining our roles. Don't you agree?"

She hardly gave Sharon the chance to answer before she started in on Doris Pitts. "Everyone is wondering why you haven't done something about that woman. All of my girls keep asking me why she never has to take a turn at rotation. What can I tell them? And how can you expect Laurie Canaday to do her job when you keep such an uncooperative employee on her unit? Do you think that's fair?"

"Keeping Pitts on an easy ward was not my doing," Sharon answered.

"I know it wasn't, but you're in charge now. What are you afraid of?"

"I'm not afraid," Sharon protested, feeling increasingly more helpless.

Then Faith went on to mention Mathilda Hoxie's malicious gossip, hinting that it was Sharon's responsibility to shut her up. Sharon knew it would take a miracle of rebirth to make Mathilda Hoxie stop talking!

As soon as Faith left Sharon's office, she went straight to Rick Armstrong's office to repeat her conversation with Sharon, and to report that Sharon was obviously losing her grip, and that she didn't have enough of the cool-headed professionalism that it took to be a competent Director of Nurses. She also told Rick that Sharon and Laurie both seemed to have a grudge against Doris Pitts.

"Well, I certainly appreciate your sharing all of this with me," Rick said. "I do agree that Sharon should schedule more staff meetings. And I'm beginning to wonder..."

He stopped himself from saying what was on his mind, since he didn't want to give Faith the impression that he was having doubts as to Sharon's ability. But he had the feeling that he should check more deeply into Sharon's role, to see if she was indeed competent enough to satisfy the demanding requirements of such an important position.

"To satisfy the demanding requirements..." he thought, closing the door after Faith had left and popping a peanut into his mouth. For a minute or two, he didn't want to think about the demands of running the Institution. No, he just wanted to daydream for a while about the beautiful, sexy Rene Boutelle, who hadn't been as available to him as she used to be.

"I do miss her, though," he thought, smacking his lips unconsciously at the thought of her. And he was just about to remember the last tryst they'd had together when someone was knocking firmly on his door.

It was Laurie, and she broke the ice right away, by asking him how he felt about sexual activity on the wards.

"Do you think we can condone it when we have no way of determining if both parties are consenting?"

"That depends on who's throwing the party!" he said, chuckling at his own little joke.

Laurie sat up straighter in her chair and could feel the tenseness building up in her back and shoulder muscles.

"This isn't anything to joke about, Rick," she said.

"But obviously we can't condone anything like that," Rick said, chewing the last of his peanuts. "Whoever said we could?"

"Randy Sinclair, that's who," Laurie said. "It came up in an A-6 treatment-team meeting which Corbett called to help us find ways to eliminate the behavior, but Randy said it should be done in a private place, such as the bathroom, in the last stall. That was his suggestion for dealing with the problem -- hiding it!"

"But that's absurd," Rick said.

"Well, I'm glad to hear that you agree with me. But Randy didn't agree. He called me an asshole with hangups, right in front of everybody. Rick, couldn't you straighten him out and tell him how you feel about it?"

Rick may have agreed with Laurie about the issue, but he certainly wasn't willing to speak to Randy about it.

"Listen," he said, in an irritated voice, "you've got to tell him yourself, Laurie. It's part of your job as coordinator. Don't you see that you'd be neutralizing your own power, if you call me in on your problems?"

"Oh, I see," Laurie said, swallowing her pride. So he wasn't going to help her on this particular point. Well, maybe he'd be more helpful on the matter of Doris Pitts, she thought. But he wasn't. He took the exact same attitude, telling Laurie that she should deal with Pitts herself.

And when it came to the matter of Randy Sinclair's manipulating to deny Lucy Bradley's transfer to Doris Pitts's ward, even though it was Rick's policy that a socially-aware patient should never be held back on a bed ward simply because she was in a wheelchair, he said, using his most obscure technical interpretations of the English language, "Laurie, you need to dilute the polarization of your staff. The Unit Chief should coordinate and harness the various views in an environment of constructive rehabilitation, focusing primarily on the residents' needs."

"Oh, really?" she said. "Is that so? Gee, I would have said the same thing myself, if I'd understood any of it!! But you haven't told me how I should go about doing it!"

"Let Pitts stay and give her a chance to fail," Rick said, by way of translation. "If she doesn't perform, write it up on her next evaluation, and we'll get rid of her. You just tell her that her ward ain't no sanctuary, and that it can be pissed on the same as any other ward in this place."

Then Laurie brought up the last but not the least item of concern to her -- Rene Boutelle. Without realizing that she was hitting a very sore spot in Rick's armor, she said, "That woman is upsetting everyone with her insults and condescending attitude. And the worst thing about it is that you did not post that job before you gave it to her. Since she is just creating conflict in my unit, I would like to request that you move her out of that position."

"I'm afraid I can't comply with your request, Laurie," he said. "One of the main functions of a Unit Chief is to conduct an ongoing review process and to assess and advise the staff on their effectiveness. It's similar to a quality control job, and is an absolutely necessary, even essential part of the smooth operation of the entire Institution. Maybe you could arrange a meeting with the team leaders to help clarify Rene's role and responsibilities."

He seemed to be finished with his little speech, and finished with Laurie, who left his office, feeling not only that she had gained nothing, but also that something precious had been taken from her. Trying to sort out her feelings, she realized that she was out on a limb, all by herself, and wondered if all her hopes for making a difference in the lives of the patients, would just turn into dust.

Nathan Strenge's plans for 'unitization' became reality. He had successfully decentralized the Main Building, dissolving the authority of the powerful Nursing Director. Grace Maybury was relegated to the position of Advisor and Consultant.

But Grace Maybury had no intentions of taking this lying down.

As members of Strenge's PERU team assumed control of the respective units, the positions of the nurse supervisors also became irrelevant.

It was his contention that, since Dunton was a mental institution and not a hospital, a strong nursing presence was not appropriate.

For the time being, Nathan Strenge had successfully "broken the back of the nursing stronghold" in the Main Building.

However, with the decline in the nursing influence, came the decline in the quality of patient care.

When Jessica Gray, formerly a supervisor, now relegated to administering medications, went to give patient Hattie Carlson her four o'clock dose of insulin, she found her locked in a tray chair, her head bent forward, and her body slumped lifelessly to one side. She lifted Hattie's head to see if she was conscious, but Hattie didn't respond at all; her skin was dry and her face flushed.

"Get the doctor on call immediately!" Jessica shouted to the nearest aide. Addressing the aide in charge of the ward, she said, "Why is this patient locked in a tray chair?"

"She was already in there when I came on duty," the aide answered. "I was told that she was really 'acting out,' staggering around, not wanting to get off her bed, so she was put in this tray chair."

"Acting out?" Jesssica said, trying not to scream although she was furious. "Did she eat any lunch?"

"No," the aide said. "She wasn't given anything to eat as a punishment for her bad behavior. No, I don't mean 'punishment.' That's not a word we're supposed to use. But she wasn't given any token to buy her lunch -- whatever you want to call that."

"Well, good God!" Jessica said, her voice rising in spite of her efforts to control it. "For your information, this patient wasn't 'acting out,' or pretending not to want to get up off her bed. She was having an insulin reaction, further complicated by the fact that she hasn't eaten. And as of right now, she isn't responding at all. Do you have any idea how serious this is?"

At that moment, Dr. Gallino entered the ward and examined the patient. "When was the last time this patient had insulin?" he said, recognizing her condition immediately. "She's in shock!"

"She had protamine zinc insulin at six this morning," Jessica told him. "Her clinitest at eleven A.M. was negative, so she didn't receive insulin then. From what I understand, her 'acting out' and staggering around started just before lunchtime."

"Just about the right time for a reaction to protamine zinc," the doctor said. We'll have to give her glucose intravenously. Prepare a 50cc ampule."

Jessica assisted the doctor, then helped the aides put Hattie to bed, and stayed with her until she began to respond and her condition stabilized. And all the while she sat with her, Jessica cringed at the thought of what could have happened.

"Mrs. Maybury is going to hear about this!" she promised herself. "Hattie could have died! And then would the shit have hit the fan!"

Nathan Strenge issued a memo to Rick Armstrong which was in keeping with his goal to extend his program throughout the entire Institution. As Rick read it, his face turned beet red, and the words seemed to jump up at him, grabbing him by the throat:

A behavior modification program is now in operation in the Main Building. This experimental program is aimed at raising the level of functioning in a group of regressed and disturbed patients, many of whom are combative and destructive.

As of this date, an extension of the program will go into effect at the Annex. Our aim is to promote a level of self-care and patient-staff cooperation compatible with adjustment to placement in the community.

To reach this goal, behavior modification in the form of token economy will be used to help the patients learn new and more successful ways of coping with life.

For this ambitious program to be successful, we need the cooperation of the entire Annex.

Please post this memo on the Bulletin Board, so that everyone will have the chance to review it.

Rick was vehemently against Behavior Modification, and he wasn't about to sacrifice his preferred treatment method -- Milieu Therapy -- in deference to those "weirdoes", as he referred to them, in the Main Building. He would do everything in his power to delay, postpone or block its introduction on his units.

CHAPTER FOURTEEN

In the Main Building, Terrance Long, a patient with a long history as a violent sex offender, had been allowed out for the first time on a 48-hour pass. When Nurse Susan Mahoney, a former supervisor, became aware that the time had come and gone for him to report back in, she began to worry, and then to panic. The account of his murder of an elderly woman was so repulsive that Susan shivered in fear and disgust just from thinking of it.

By the time he was half an hour overdue, Susan called Bart Hanson, PERU team member, in charge of Terrance's unit.

Bart was busily monitoring some psychosocial records to see that they were being properly kept, and that positive progress was being shown for the patients.

"This is Susan Mahoney," she said to him over the phone. "I'm calling to let you know that Terrance Long is half an hour overdue from his weekend leave."

"I wouldn't worry, Susan," Bart said. "He's certainly been a model patient. That's why we thought it would be a good idea to reward him with this leave in the first place."

"But he has such a terrible record that it makes me nervous to think of him at large," she said. "Maybe we should notify the police."

"The police?" he said. "No, that's a little premature, I think. Just because he has a record doesn't mean we should persecute him. I'm sure he'll be right along."

After hanging up with her, Bart shook his head in disbelief. "Can you imagine?" he said to one of his colleagues in the office, "wanting to call the police when the guy is only thirty minutes late. These nurses! I'd sure hate to be married to one. It's a whole lot easier to train aides without such hangups to be therapists!"

But Susan felt extremely uneasy as she left her ward at the end of her shift, knowing that Terrance Long was now overdue.

The police were also uneasy when they were finally notified that Terrance hadn't shown up after his leave, and that he had been granted leave at all. As the word was spread to all the city police, the police of the surrounding towns and the State police, all of them started combing the area in search of this man who had committed a gruesome murder.

When a truck driver reported that he had parked his truck with the keys in them, walking away for a minute and then returning to find that his truck had been stolen, an all-points bulletin was issued, and several hours later, more than sixty miles away, Terrance Long was finally apprehended, driving under the influence of alcohol.

There was a general outrage over the incident, especially in the State's Attorney General's office, which had unsuccessfully prosecuted Long in the first place, due to his plea of insanity. And the outrage was so great that it led to the speedy passage into law of a bill prohibiting Institution officials from granting any leaves for court-committed individuals.

Nathan Strenge, Zeb Ramsey, and Bart Hanson came under fire for their "lack of responsibility to the public, and total disregard of the community," in allowing Terrance Long to go out on leave.

At the Annex, the morale continued to sink as ward staff were buried knee-deep in paper, trying to fulfill their obligation of dealing with that intricate psychosocial record-keeping system that was taking so much time away from their patients.

If a patient had four problem behaviors, with two techniques for correcting each, that would amount to having to write up eight progress reports each week, just on that one patient. But what appeared on the records seldom reflected what was really going on, if anything, with the patients

One afternoon, as A-2 team leader, Faye Garland, found herself buried in paper, she said to the evening aide coming to relieve her, "The patients' charts are getting so stuffed with forms that it takes me forever just to find the one I want. I'm looking for the progress sheet for technique number two (restrict patient to the ward) for behavior number one (patient curses) to chart the progress, if any, being made. Let's see," she went on, "the last progress report stated that Harry is cursing half an hour a day."

"How about showing that his cursing has decreased to fifteen minutes twice a week?" the evening aide suggested.

"But that wouldn't leave much room for progress the next time," Faye argued. "I think I'll let the record show that his cursing had decreased to fifteen minutes a day.

"Be sure you chart it on the progress sheet for technique number two for behavior number one, and not on the one for technique number one for behavior number two. Last week Corbett did that, and she didn't get a very good grade on her records."

"Gee, I'll try not to make that mistake," Faye said, grinning. "We certainly wouldn't want to get anything so important all screwed up, now would we?"

Grace Maybury and Lula Bagley were lamenting their sad state of affairs. But Grace was not going to let Strenge keep her out of control. She wasn't going to sit still for that.

"We couldn't be luckier that Strenge and his crew are in the soup now," Maybury said, a cruel, vengeful smile curling at the corners of her mouth. "In fact, now would be a good time to strike, Bagley, while the iron's hot."

"It says here in the newspaper that the Comptroller is perplexed by the concurrent rise in payroll and drop in patient census at this Institution. Well, I could clear up his perplexity in a damned hurry! I'm gonna write a letter, and I think I'll get Randy to help me do it."

"A letter to the commissioner?" Bagley asked excitedly.

"To hell with the commissioner?" Maybury declared. "I'm goin' to the top. The Governor's the one who's been tryna shut this place down and consolidate the institutions. Hell, I'd rather see it shut down than turned over to Strenge and his gang. Yeah, I think I'll get that highly gifted and prolific Randy Sinclair over here right away. He'll jump at the chance to run off at the mouth, or at the pen, as the case may be."

She was right, of course. As soon as Randy heard the words, he exclaimed, "Could I write a letter? That's my thing! If it'll help get those bastards out of here, it will be well worth my time. I'll be right over."

So Maybury and Randy, having his own ax to grind, worked diligently composing their letter, of which the main points were as follows:

...the Institution is not treatment-oriented as claimed, and a large number of the administrative staff does not have any

138

contact with the patients. The record-keeping system has overburdened and frustrated the ward staff, taking them away from giving attention to their patients.

The Skilled-Care unit, only half full, has a ratio of four staff members for eight patients, and the accepted policy has been to search for patients to justify keeping the unit open. Based on the prohibitive cost of keeping this unit operational, it would certainly be more economically feasible to send patients to the general hospital for treatment.

Although they hesitated to bring up the fact that Nathan Strenge had given his wife a high-salaried position, and that she was rarely ever seen, they decided to go ahead and let all their cannons fire. They went into detail about how Strenge fired an attendant for insubordination when the attendant had simply asked if it was necessary for Mrs. Strenge to keep attending workshops, thereby making herself chronically absent from the hospital.

"Well, that oughta give the Governor something to think about!" Randy said, admiring his accomplishment.

"I hope he won't just think about it, Randy, but act on it too!" Grace said, placing the letter in an envelope and addressing it to the State House.

Sharon Lovejoy was becoming more and more depressed. She was losing her old self-confidence. It was evident in her vacant expression, in her step which had become slow and dragging, and in her eyes which had lost their sparkle.

When she and Laurie met in her office to begin working on their own new job descriptions as well as those of their staff, as Rick had instructed, reflecting his goals and his program, she told Laurie that she couldn't seem to do anything right anymore.

"Don't lose your enthusiasm now, Sharon," Laurie said, anxiously, "I need you on my side. And what makes you think you can't do anything right anymore?"

"Faith Byrd seems to think she needs to hound me constantly," Sharon complained, and everything she says makes its own kind of sense, but I just can't go along with all of her 'proposals' and 'suggestions'."

"Well, what are they? What does she think you should do?" Laurie asked.

"The latest is that she wants me to institute a CPR policy, but because the doctors won't specify in writing which patients are not to be 'coded', if we do have a CPR policy, we'll have to attempt to resuscitate every patient, even the terminally-ill, unless they are found dead."

" 'They should make that decision for every patient, and it's your responsibility to insist that they put it in writing,' Faith says. 'Do you think it's fair to leave that decision to the nurse? What if a nurse finds herself with a cardiac arrest? Where does that leave her?'"

"Faith says these things to me, and then she always ends up by saying, 'Do you think it's fair?'"

Sharon cupped her head between the palms of her hands, and staring absent-mindedly, went on.

"I don't believe in resuscitating terminally-ill patients, banging and pounding on their chests. Do you believe we should allow them to die in peace, with dignity, Laurie, or do you think Faith's right?"

These questions were far too complex for Laurie to try to solve. She could have suggested bringing them up at a team meeting, but the team leaders were so angry about the manipulation that was going on in team meetings, that they weren't calling them anymore.

So Laurie said, "I don't know, one way or the other, but I want you to know that I'm here for you, and that you can talk to me whenever you want, Sharon. Do you understand?"

"Yes, I understand," Sharon said.

It seemed to Laurie that Sharon was fighting against something buried deep inside her. And that she was defending herself as if someone had charged her with being inadequate. But Sharon wasn't inadequate... she was just tired.

"I think you're taking Faith too seriously," Laurie said. "I'm sure she doesn't mean things the way they sound. She's just very enthusiastic. Cheer up, Sharon. Things will work out."

But Laurie wasn't so sure that they would. She knew that Sharon was getting irritable a lot lately, and ready to jump at anyone, even if they were trying to lend her a helping hand. And besides, Faith Byrd couldn't possibly be as threatening as Sharon was suggesting. She was just trying to do her job, that was all.

"I'd better keep an eye on Sharon, just in case," Laurie thought, as they commenced working on the job descriptions, "because the poor thing seems to be falling apart at the seams."

Rene Boutelle was on Doris Pitts's ward, working on some patient treatment plans, when social worker Dorothy Sterns entered the A-3 chartroom.

"I've found boarding-home placement," Dorothy said, consulting the clipboard in her hand, and leafing through some pages until she found the one she was looking for, "for three of your patients, Mrs. Pitts -- Dora Kuntz, Minnie Spencer, and Pearl Higgins. The color drained from Pitts's face as she thought, "Not my best patients. You're not going to take my three best patients away from me."

But it looked as if that was exactly what she wanted to do. Jolting Pitts from her bewilderment, Dorothy continued. "If these patients were to be discharged, that would create room for your patient Alma Foss, who's ready to return from having her colostomy."

"But how could she come back so soon?" Doris said, dreading the idea of colostomy irrigations.

"Oh, there's no problem with the colostomy," Dorothy assured her. "All it requires is routine care."

"I really don't know about the other three patients," Pitts said hesitantly. "I don't think it would be a good idea to move them, since they've been here for so many years. They'd have a real bad time adjusting to the 'outside.'"

"I'm sure there would be some adjustment time for them," Dorothy said, "but it would be a marvelous opportunity for them, don't you think? They deserve the chance of making new lives for themselves after all these years. Anyway, I've asked Laurie Canaday to coordinate a team meeting for next week so that we can all discuss the appropriateness of the move."

Rene, who'd been sitting quietly throughout the whole conversation, didn't speak until Dorothy Sterns had left the room.

"Why don't you call Randy?" she said.

"That's exactly what I intend to do," Doris said, dialing the phone and starting to shout into it. "They're tryna make a dumpin' ground out of my ward again, and you'd better do somethin' about it!"

"I know what we can do," Rene whispered, and when Randy came to meet with them, she told them her plan. It was really quite simple -- just to talk to the three patients involved, and ask them how they'd feel about being sent away -- kicked out of the Institution.

As the three patients assembled in the chartroom, Rene said, "We just wanted to let you know that you won't be staying here much longer. Poor things, we feel sorry for you, but there's nothing we can do about it."

"What do you mean?" Dora said. "Why won't we be staying here anymore?"

"Because they've decided to kick you out." Doris said.

"Kick us out?" Dora said, frightened and trying not to cry.

"But how can they do that to us? We haven't done anything wrong, have we? Did we do something terrible? Do they really hate us now, or want to punish us?"

"No, they don't hate you," Rene said. "And you haven't done anything wrong. In fact, you haven't done anything that would give you a reason to stay. The plain truth is that the rules are all different now. They have to have a good reason to keep patients here."

"What are some of the reasons to keep a patient here?" Pearl asked, "some of the reasons why other patients can stay?"

"Some of them wet their beds at night, or holler and roam around after lights-out, or destroy property or try to run away," Randy said. "No place on the 'outside' will accept or keep a patient like that, so that's why they can stay here."

"I have no place to go," Minnie said, tightly rolling a handkerchief in her lap. "Where would I go?"

"They'll put you someplace," Pitts said, "but I don't know where, or what it'll be like. I'm not even sure if you'll be able to have your things with you. Some places don't let patients have anything."

"When do we have to go?" Dora asked.

"We'll be having a meeting about it next week sometime," Rene said, "and if they can't find any reasons like the ones just mentioned for you to stay, then you'll have to go."

"Oh, thank you for telling us!" they all said, looking at each other in despair.

Unfortunately for the conspirators, and unknown to them, Margaret Putnam, the three-to-eleven aide on Pitts's ward had come on duty a little early that day, and overheard every word that was said.

"We've added CPR teams for every shift now," Sharon told eleven-to-seven supervisor, June Buck, during a morning shift report. "It was one of Faith Byrd's suggestions, and I had to follow through on it, since she convinced Rick that there was a need for it. She thinks I should demand from the doctors that they indicate in writing which patients should and should not be 'coded'. Can you imagine me demanding anything of the doctors?"

"She doesn't give a damn," said Buck, "all she wants is to shoot her mouth off to make herself look better than the rest of us."

"I'm really dreading to have the next patient die and have to go through that performance," Laurie said, with great anxiety." "It seems so dehumanizing and cruel to bring back a terminally- ill old patient for a few more hours of discomfort. I wish there were some way we could get out of it."

"I know how to get out of it!" June said. "CPR is to be done only when the patient's death is witnessed. It can't be done on a patient who is *found* dead, because there wouldn't be any way of knowing when he lost his vital signs. My people will all get the message that from now on, any patient who dies will be found dead. I'll never," June continued, "let anyone suspect that a patient's death was witnessed, because of the legal implications of not doing CPR. No Faith Byrd will ever get me to do that. I'll get out of nursing first!"

CHAPTER FIFTEEN

Sharon wrote and submitted her letter of resignation that same day. In it, she said only that she was leaving to take some time off for a while, but there was a lot more that she didn't say. She didn't say that it was impossible to work under the present conditions. She didn't say how senseless she thought all the paperwork was, how futile and unnecessary, how shameful.

But shame was the word she used when she told Laurie why she was quitting, because Laurie was the only person she could be completely honest with.

She and Laurie were standing in the parking lot late that afternoon. The warm March sun, staying out longer and longer every day, was just setting over the hill as the two young women watched it go, with some sadness, as if they were witnessing the passing of an old friend.

"I hope you're making the right decision," Laurie said. "I'm sure going to miss you, and I don't want to sound selfish, but I wish you'd change your mind."

"I hate to sound like I know what's going to happen," Sharon said, but there's something dangerous under the surface now, and I feel it's going to break out soon, causing a lot of grief to a lot of people. And you'd better watch out for yourself too, Laurie, because that woman -- and you know who I mean -- that evil bitch is like a barracuda swimming underwater, and she'll get you too in the end."

"What will you do, Sharon?" Laurie asked.

"I'll be here two more weeks, and after that I think I could do anything."

News of Sharon's resignation traveled quickly over the efficient grapevine. When Faith heard the news, she didn't waste any time, going immediately to Rick's office.

"Have you considered a replacement for Sharon yet?" she asked, barging in the door.

"My God," Rick said. "The woman isn't dead yet, but you've already got her buried!"

"I know I have less experience and seniority than most of the nurses in this Institution," she said, "but I consider myself best qualified for the position."

"Oh, really," Rick said. "Your bid will certainly be considered."

"And have you and Rene been meeting as often as you used to, now that she's working days?" she said, sneering at him. "I wonder how your wife would feel if she knew all about what you have been doing with Rene."

For one of the few times in his life, Rick was speechless.

"I really think we should change the title of that position to Assistant Administrator," Faith continued. "I would like to get away from that 'nursing' image. It sounds so feminine."

Rick remained silent.

"You won't be disappointed," she said, turning on her heels and walking out the door.

They were clustered in small groups in the Activity Area, talking quietly among themselves, the nurses and aides whom Sharon had known throughout her years at Dunton, some having come over from the Main Building, waiting for her to arrive so they could celebrate her last day of work. When Laurie entered the room, she stopped here and there to say hello to everyone, on her way to the long table where refreshments had been laid out. And although she kept hearing the name Faith Byrd as she walked through the room, Faith herself was conspicuous by her absence.

When Sharon walked into the room, it was clear that she'd been crying, and people rushed up to her, making a circle around her, patting her on the arm and saying how sad they were to see her go. It was enough to make the more emotional among them shed a tear or two, and Sharon nodded, saying, "Thanks, I'll miss you too."

As Sharon finally made her way to Laurie, Rick Armstrong walked in with a woman they hadn't seen before. He stood stiffly in the middle of the room and said "Ahem" a few times very loudly to get everyone's attention, and soon the room had grown quiet enough for him to begin his speech. The small young woman was still standing next to him, and all eyes were fixed on her.

"As we all know," Rick began, "we are here to say good-bye to one of our favorite people -- Sharon Lovejoy. I am certainly going to miss Sharon. She has been devoted, hard-working, and wonderful to work with. Sharon, where are you? Will you step forward please, so everyone can see you?"

Sharon stood up and nodded gravely at the faces around her.

"And now," Rick was saying, "I'd like to introduce you all to Joan Decker. Joan will be replacing Faith Byrd as Medical Unit B Chief. For those of you who do not as yet know, I would like to announce that Faith will be moving up to the Assistant Administrator position, replacing Sharon."

Some of the more qualified nurses were muttering under their breath. Others were shaking their heads, angry and upset, but feeling helpless, since there was nothing they could do to change things. It was already too late for that.

Even though Sharon's position had been posted, Rick had put out the word so quickly that Faith was his choice as a replacement, that no one else had even bothered to apply, knowing full well they would be rejected.

Joan Decker was a nurse in her early thirties, an attractive woman with brown hair and dark brown eyes, who appeared to be intelligent and astute. She had a warm smile, and Laurie hoped that they could become friends, because she knew she was going to feel alone, once Sharon was gone.

At that very moment, Faith Byrd entered the room. She wouldn't have stayed away for a million dollars, and although hardly anyone spoke to her, she had a gloating, sneering look on her face that made Sharon want to kill her.

"Listen, Laurie," Sharon said, "I can't stay here now, so I'm going over to say good-bye to Rick. Will you come with me to my office, for the last time, so I can clear out my belongings?"

"I'd be happy to go with you," Laurie said, standing up and walking with Sharon over to Rick and Faith. As they approached, they could just hear Rick saying, "It's going to be great having you to work with."

"I thought I was supposed to be wonderful to work with," Sharon said, kiddingly, "devoted and hard-working, and all of that."

"Oh, that was just for the troops," Rick said, brushing Sharon off and turning a cold shoulder on her.

It seemed to hit Sharon like a physical blow, as if Rick had slapped her, and Laurie could see Sharon crumbling on the spot. But she didn't cry until they were safely out of the Activity Area, until they had closed the door to her office.

"I hate to leave this place and these patients in Faith's hands," she said when she had calmed down enough to speak. "She's so cold-hearted and scheming. She doesn't even want my job. My job is just chicken feed to her. What she really wants is to get to the top. My job is just another stepping stone."

"I'm sorry you feel that way," Laurie said. "But Faith couldn't be as bad as you make her out to be."

Sharon looked at Laurie quizzically, as if she were trying to analyze how serious Laurie's comment had been. "You don't see it, do you? You're too naive to imagine how anyone could be so ruthless, so ambitious. But you'll only get hurt in the end, Laurie, if you don't face the ugly facts. Please be careful."

As she started pulling open the drawers of her desk and emptying things into a cardboard box, she said, "You know something, I should have seen it coming. I always had the feeling that something was going on, but I couldn't put my finger on it. I used to wonder all the time why she was verbally attacking me, coming in almost on a daily basis to jump all over me with her words.

"But all of a sudden, now that I'm on my way out the door, I can see things clearly. If only I'd realized what she was doing, I'd have taken a leave of absence. If only I'd known what a power monger she was, she'd never have gotten my position for a springboard."

"She may be ambitious, Sharon, but I don't think she's out to get me. I don't think she was out to get you either. It just...happened that way."

"It didn't just happen," Sharon said. She was bending over the box with a book in her hand, and she stood frozen in the same position for what seemed like the longest time. Then she said, "You still don't really believe what I've been saying, do you, Laurie?"

"I just feel bad, that's all," Laurie said. She couldn't understand Sharon's attitude, as she hugged her friend good-bye, and then watched in grieved silence as she took off her nurse's cap, folded it neatly and packed it away.

Grace Maybury's secretary walked into her boss's office with a very special letter in her hands. She knew it was special by the name of the upper left corner of the envelope, where the name of the Governor was printed in big bold letters.

As Grace tore open the envelope, her hands were shaking so badly she could hardly see the words.

> *Dear Mrs. Maybury:*
>
> *Thank you for your letter in regard to what you see as a surplus of high-echelon staff at Dunton Mental Institution, and expressing your concern for the role of nurses.*
>
> *I have shared the information you have given us with the Commissioner of Mental Health and Corrections, so he may have the benefit of your firsthand experience with this situation. Please know that a study group from the Department has been established to investigate the conditions you described, and to report back to me as expeditiously as possible.*
>
> *Thank you again for bringing this matter to my attention.*

And it was signed "Sincerely", by the Governor himself.

Grace called Lula and Randy right away, to celebrate. "So it's finally coming to pass," Maybury said. "And now the Governor is sending us a study group to investigate. Oh, it's just too wonderful for words!"

"Yeah," Randy said, "but I wonder just how much the study group will unearth, once they start digging."

As the three conspirators looked at each other, they all began to wonder how much responsibility they had taken on, and whether or not they might actually have helped in digging their own graves.

CHAPTER SIXTEEN

It was time for the A-3 team meeting to discuss the proposed discharges of Dora Kuntz, Minnie Spencer, and Pearl Higgins.

"I have found a place with accommodations for all three of them," social worker Dorothy Sterns began. It's a lovely place in a country setting, and since they are good friends and behave so acceptably, they could continue being together, which I think will be a wonderful opportunity for them."

"Speaking of acceptable behavior," Rene said, "do homes accept patients who are incontinent?"

"Oh, no," Dorothy said.

"Well, I've been receiving reports from the night shift," Doris Pitts said, "that Minnie Spencer and Dora Kuntz have been incontinent."

"I'm really surprised to hear that," Betsy Dunn, the Activity Director, said. "I've never known either of those patients to be incontinent."

"I was surprised to hear it too," Laurie said, "in morning report. I'd never been aware of it in the past. Have they been given extra fluids before going to bed?" she asked Pitts.

"No, they haven't," she answered abruptly.

Then Randy spoke up. "I guess that in view of this intermittent night-time incontinence, it wouldn't be appropriate for them to go out at this time. Perhaps they can be re-evaluated at a later date."

"Well, shall we discuss Pearl Higgins now?" asked Dorothy Sterns.

"I would like to say here," replied Randy, "that Pearl is subject to episodes of severe depression."

Doris Pitts nodded, and said, "As a matter of fact, she was heard saying that she wants to die, a few nights ago. Maybe that's the reason she was trying to run away."

"Run away?" Dorothy asked. "What in the world is going on here? When I interviewed her, she was in such a jolly mood. She is -- she was, I thought -- one of the best-adjusted patients on this ward. I don't understand what could have happened to her between the time I saw her and now. Was there a sudden death in her family, or some catastrophe to bring about such a sudden disintegration of her good spirits?"

"Not that I know of," Randy said. "She has just always had a tendency to depression, and I feel that leaving her old friends to go to a strange place would be very detrimental to her now. Therefore, I strongly recommend against moving her."

"I guess that shoots down my plans for them all," Dorothy said, disappointedly. "Although, as I said, I can't see any reasons to justify the sudden change in the behavior of all three patients. It's very bizarre, if you ask me."

"I think it's alarming too," Laurie said. "They have been model patients, in my opinion, for quite some time, helping with ward chores, working hard...which is precisely why they were on Pitts's ward to begin with. It's just a strange turn of events, and it's a shame, really."

"It's a terrible shame for them to lose this opportunity at living a more normal kind of existence," she thought to herself as she left the room at the end of the meeting, "especially where they could all be together."

"Miss Canaday? Can I speak to you for a minute?"

"Why, certainly, Margaret," Laurie said. "What's the matter? You look...almost frightened."

"Well, I am a little scared," the young woman said in a whisper, looking over both shoulders before she continued to speak.

"Those patients were scared out of leaving," she said. "I overheard them scaring those patients last week."

"Overheard them?" Laurie said. "Who are you talking about?"

"Pitts and that girl who goes around and writes up the treatment plans, and the psychologist. I heard them talking to the patients in the chartroom just as I was coming on duty."

"What did you hear them say?" Laurie asked, leaning down closer to Margaret to hear the girl's soft voice.

"I heard Pitts tell them that they might not be able to take their own things with them, where they were going. Minnie sounded really scared, because she said she had no place to go. I guess she thought they were going to dump her out on the street somewhere!"

"So that's why they've been having all these sudden problems," Laurie thought.

"Listen, I don't want to get in any trouble for saying this," Margaret continued, "but I just had to get this off my chest."

"It was Pitts and that Sinclair guy, and the other one was Rene? Right?" asked Laurie.

"Yes, that's right. Her name is Rene Boutelle. When the patients asked them why they were being kicked out -- and those were the very words they used -- they were told that it was because they didn't do all the things that would let them stay, such as wet the bed, try to run away, and threaten to kill themselves."

"I shouldn't have been so stupid!" Laurie said. "I should have known all along. But why didn't you tell me any of this before?"

"Because I'm afraid to get into any trouble," the girl said. I work on Pitts's ward."

"Well, I do thank you for telling me, Margaret, even if it is late." And with that, she stomped down to the chartroom, her veins almost bursting with anger. Breathing quickly, and feeling her own heartbeat increase rapidly, Laurie confronted Pitts as soon as she set eyes on her.

"I have just heard about your little performance to scare those three patients into doing things to spoil their chances at leaving Dunton -- at starting new lives for themselves!" she said in a loud, stern voice. "And I know why you did it too, because you want them to stay here, on your ward, taking care of themselves, doing your chores and filling slots to keep some other patients out, who might require some care. Well, and you listen carefully to me, because I'm only going to say this once: I AM GOING TO SEE TO IT THAT YOU ARE REMOVED FROM THIS UNIT, and your partners in this will also be dealt with. Do you understand me? Do you hear what I'm telling you?"

Laurie didn't even give Pitts a chance to answer before she spun around and stomped off the ward.

It was at the shift change, and after giving a quick, sharp look to Margaret Putnam, Doris Pitts went straight downstairs to Randy Sinclair's office to tell him what had just happened.

"There's nothing to worry about," Randy said, trying to reassure her. "Laurie Canaday can't remove you from your ward if Rick disapproves. And from the way Rene's been bragging about having him whenever she wants, I'd say we have a pretty good weapon to use against him. I'm sure he wouldn't want his wife to know about his shenanigans. I'll go and talk to him right away, Doris, so just stop worrying, okay?"

Thinking that he would have to get to Rick Armstrong before Laurie did, Randy went straight to Rick's office, setting all his cards on the table.

"I suppose you've heard that there's been some conflict between Laurie and Doris Pitts," he said.

"Yes, I've already heard something about it," Rick said.

"Well, Laurie seems to be persecuting Doris," Randy said. "She just doesn't like her, for some reason, and neither did Sharon. Well, my point is this. When Doris found out that three of her patients were going to be transferred, she asked them if they wanted to leave, and they were terrified at the idea. Maybe it wasn't strictly correct for us to talk to them while their discharges were still in the proposal stage, but Doris and Rene and I went to talk to the three patients to put their minds at ease. We were shocked to find that they were so distressed at the news, that their behavior began to regress.

"Apparently one of the aides heard us, and related our conversation to Laurie, and she -- that neurotic woman -- stormed into the chartroom to tell Doris that she would try to have her removed from the unit, after all her years of service. It's just ridiculous."

"From the way it sounds, this is serious enough for Laurie to come to me personally," said Rick. "I will listen to her side of the story before I make any decisions."

"Oh, by the way," Randy said, stiffly, "I want to congratulate you on getting so far with that hot young stuff. Rene tells me you're quite a man. I wonder if your wife would agree."

Randy could see right away that he'd played his trump card. Rick's face grew pale, as if the blood had suddenly been drained out of it.

"Well, I'm sure you'll arrive at the right decision," Randy said, getting up and leaving Rick's office with all of his confidence and hopes for the future left intact.

Rick sat at his desk, motionless, staring into his visions of what would happen next, and trying to figure out why Randy would go to so much trouble for that bitch Doris Pitts, who was getting to be such a thorn in Rick's side. He knew that Laurie would be coming in, demanding to be allowed to remove Pitts from her unit...but this was a demand that Rick Armstrong simply couldn't meet, and neither could he explain to Laurie why his hands were tied.

The next day, when Laurie came, as Rick had predicted, she presented her side of the picture in a straightforward, determined manner.

"Yesterday I learned that Doris Pitts, Rene Boutelle and Randy Sinclair collaborated to sabotage the discharges of three patients, by meeting with them before the team meeting, scaring them about the move, and then implying what they could do to destroy their chances for leaving."

Rick thought that the word "sabotage" was a bit over-dramatic, but that was definitely Laurie's point of view.

"The three patients then accommodated them," she continued, "by exhibiting the appropriate 'inappropriate' behaviors, which were used at the meeting to deny their discharges. Now I need you to speak to Randy about this unethical conduct, and transfer the other two staff out of my unit."

Rick sighed painfully, and said, "I will write a memo to be put in their records, reprimanding each for discussing with patients discharge plans which are still in the proposal stage."

"Didn't you hear what I just said," she asked, spitting out each word. "They obstructed the discharges of three patients for selfish reasons, because they are self-care and want to prevent having to fill their vacancies with other patients who might require care. Do you think that's right.? Whatever happened to your commitment to upgrade patient care? Whatever happened to your grand goals and objectives?"

"I think you're under a lot of pressure, Laurie," he said. "I've seen the strain in your eyes and in your face lately. I wish I knew how to help you, but frankly, I'm getting pretty tired of hearing all of your petty complaints. I guess I'm just one of those people who don't like to listen to gossip."

"But this isn't gossip, Rick! It's...why, it's totally unethical, and I can't see how you can allow such underhanded behavior to go on. Why won't you support me by allowing me to transfer Pitts off my unit? She is undermining your goals and your program, and she is frustrating my efforts to do the work I'm committed to doing."

"It seems to me, Laurie, that you're just creating your own problems by reinforcing negative feelings in your staff."

"Reinforcing negative feelings!" she said, hating the sound of the behaviorist terminology, which had found its way into almost everyone's speech, even Rick's, being applied to her.

"My staff wants to meet with you," she said. "They want some answers. They're angry and they're demanding that this Doris Pitts situation be dealt with."

"Then you should deal with it," Rick said, as he had told her before. "If they see me sticking my nose into your affairs, it would only undermine your efforts, your strength as a Unit Chief. So you need to pull your staff together."

"Then you are refusing to support me?" she asked.

"If you call me in on your problems," he said again, infuriating her by repeating himself, "then you'll only be neutralizing your own power."

"My own power," she said, suddenly losing all the emotional tenor, the vitality, in her voice.

Then, in a calm, matter-of-fact way, she said, "I have brought to your attention facts that I feel you should act upon. For some reason, unknown to me, you cannot or will not even investigate them. I see that I am wasting my time attempting to communicate with you."

Laurie stood up, but before she walked out, she said, bursting with anger, "Be assured of one thing, Mr. do-nothing, I will not compromise my standards, not for you or anyone else in this madhouse!"

When she was physically out the door, Rick Armstrong took a swig from his bottle of antacid and pressed his hands deeply into his epigastrium to try to relieve the agonizing, gnawing pain in his abdomen.

"Why can't she just leave things alone? If Kathy ever finds out about Rene, I'll lose her. She wouldn't forgive me this time. And oh God," he thought, as he lifted his bottle to his mouth for another gulp, remembering a compulsory Geriatric Advisory Committee meeting scheduled in the Main Building for that afternoon.

"How can I go over there? They'll tear me apart. I haven't instituted their pet program, and I know Strenge and Ramsey are gunnin' for me. I'd like to analyze them sometime and get them declared 'non compos mentis'!

"If I go to that meeting, they'll string me up for sure. Oh, if only someone could go in my place and stand in for me. Maybe, just maybe Faith would do this little favor for me."

CHAPTER SEVENTEEN

As it turned out, as Rick had hoped, Faith was more than happy to attend the meeting in his place. Since she had set her sights on the highest peak, she knew she must use every opportunity to make her presence known in the Main Building. And there was no time like the present, she believed, especially when she could put Rick at the disadvantage of sending a woman to do his work for him.

She knew that it wouldn't look good for Rick, but that the opposite would be true for her. Yes, she wanted Rick to like her -- that is, until he was of no further use to her. And she wanted Zeb Ramsey to like her too...

So she went, with hat in hand, or rather, with Rick's hat in her hand, and said in her <u>sweet</u> voice that he was too sick now to attend the meeting.

"He should have come to speak for himself," Zeb said, impatiently. "That man has been doing his own thing in the Annex for too long, completely ignoring our orders. Just who does he think he is, that he doesn't have to obey or account to his superiors?"

"Please don't be too hard on him," Faith said, wanting to make Rick sound like a little boy who's been playing hooky and doesn't want to go to school anymore. "He's having so many problems -- more problems than he can deal with!"

"And what problems are those?" asked Zeb, seeming to share Faith's delight in the fact that Rick was in some kind of trouble, and that he didn't know how to deal with it.

"Well," Faith began, settling back in her chair and relishing the moment, "there is a great deal of frustration and anger among the staff and Chief of Unit A, Laurie Canaday, because Rick won't allow the removal of an insubordinate aide, Doris Pitts. She has always received preferential treatment for some mysterious reason, and has now defied the new goals and program, and stymied the operation of the entire unit."

"That sounds like a description of Rick Armstrong!" Zeb said, "so I can see they have a lot in common."

"The staff is demanding a meeting with him to deal with this matter, and to re-establish his goals and objectives, and he refuses to meet with them. So obviously, they've lost their confidence and respect for him."

"Obviously!" Zeb said. "I would expect the same from my staff members, if I ignored their most basic wishes."

"But that isn't all," Faith said. "And this is where it gets a little sticky. There's a rumor going around that he's gotten himself involved with one of the young aides. He has even created a very special position for her, making all the other aides angry and jealous. Now you can't imagine how that is undermining the operation of the unit. It's making him literally sick; he has ulcers and hemorrhoids. And in fact, that's why he asked me to attend this meeting today in his place -- he's just too ill to face another set of responsibilities, the poor man."

Then in her <u>sweetest</u> voice with the most innocent expression on her face, she said, beseechingly, "Please tell me what I can do to help. I would really appreciate it if you would give me some direction as to how I can help this poor man. And please take it easy on him; he's practically falling apart!"

"Practically falling apart!" Zeb Ramsey thought. "Then he'll be that much easier to push over, when the time comes." He thought he recognized a new look in Faith's eyes, a come-hither glance, that he found most attractive.

He was very close to the top, and could be of use to Faith in strengthening her position. By getting into his inner circle, she could absorb some of his power.

"Yes," she told herself, leaving Zeb Ramsey's office after the meeting, "It will be well worth my time to cultivate him."

Those three patients of Doris Pitts were causing more trouble than they could have ever realized. Since their beds hadn't become vacant, Pitts's patient, Alma Foss, who'd had the colostomy, had to be returned to A-4, due to a pre-arranged lack of room on Pitts's ward, A-3.

That infuriated the A-4 staff -- not because they had a colostomy to care for, but because they were having to pick up the tab for what Doris Pitts was not required to do.

"We're being made damn fools of," A-4 team leader, Linda Bryant, complained to Laurie, "and we think you should try again to get Rick to meet with us," she added angrily.

"It's no use," said Laurie. "I've tried to communicate with him, but he won't allow it."

"Then it's time that you did something else," Linda said.

Laurie agreed.

"It is time for further action to be taken." she told herself, as she headed back to the supervisor's office. "As much as I hate to, I must go over Rick's head. I have no alternative. It is not right for him to be allowed to hold his position, when his 'position' amounts to sitting in his office, dealing with nothing."

Joan Decker was beginning to help fill the void that Laurie felt when Sharon left. She was a friendly young woman, with a sharp wit and a keen sense of humor, and was quick in opening up to Laurie, telling her exactly how she felt about everyone involved in administration at Dunton.

"Maybe you can help me write a memo to Rick Armstrong," Laurie said to her, entering the supervisor's office after her verbal exchange with the A-4 team leader. "Since I have not been very successful communicating with him verbally, maybe a written memo will get some results, since I'll be sending copies to Zeb Ramsey and Grace Maybury. There are some people that I want removed from my unit."

"Yes," Joan said, "I've already heard about that sneaky bit of business that Doris Pitts and Rene Boutelle pulled off, but don't you see, Laurie, they couldn't get away with what they're doing, if their bosses were doing their jobs.

"And where has Faith Byrd been in all of this?" Joan asked. "Rick lets her roam around here, responsible to no one, working her own hours. It's hard not to notice her and her pal Rene sauntering in here at about ten-thirty every morning, running over to the Main Building. She's supposed to be the Annex Assistant Administrator, and she spends most of her time in the Main Building, letting you wallow in your frustration."

"She's really changed since Sharon left," Laurie said. "She was always criticizing Sharon for not communicating enough with the staff, and being afraid to do anything about Doris Pitts. Now she's not even around long enough to do any communicating, and Doris Pitts is running roughshod over my unit, and her pal Rene, with Randy Sinclair, for some reason, is helping her do it."

"I want to see a copy of her job description, by God!" said Joan. "I'd like to know just how she got that job of hers, and what it entails, so I can learn how to get myself a job just like it!"

"I'd watch out for that Miss Byrd if I were you, Miss Canaday," said Dr. Bauer, the Annex physician, as he entered the office. "I think she wouldn't be too unhappy if you suddenly flew the coop."

"But why wouldn't she want me around?" asked Laurie.

"Because," Joan said, interrupting the doctor, "you're a threat to her. You're the one with the support."

"I've noticed that she spends a lot of time on your wards when you're not here," Dr. Bauer said.

"I knew this was going on," Laurie responded. "The girls have been keeping me posted. They tell me that when I'm not here, she spends a lot of time over there visiting with Rene."

"I'll help you," offered Dr. Bauer. "Give me your work schedule each week, and on your days off, I'll spend more time tripping your wards and keeping my eyes and ears open."

And Joan added, "He's right, you know. You really need to watch out for her."

"That's exactly what Sharon told me before she left," Laurie was thinking, "and I wouldn't listen to her."

CHAPTER EIGHTEEN

Writing her memo to Rick was one of the hardest things Laurie had ever done, but she found that in writing it, she was able to let out some of her rage and frustration, letting it spill over onto the pages.

Information has been brought to my attention that certain staff members collaborated before a team meeting, which was to be held for the purpose of proposing the discharges of three self-care patients, to block these discharges. This was accomplished by frightening these patients about their discharges, and then directing them as to the behaviors they could exhibit in order to destroy their chances of leaving.

The reasons for this action on the part of these staff were to retain these self-care, working patients on this ward, while preventing the creation of vacancies which could be filled by patients who might require care or might not be so hard-working.

I would like to go on record as taking a very dim view of this unethical conduct. I feel that, first of all, it undermines the patients, that secondly, it undermines me, and thirdly and most importantly, it undermines the goals and objectives, as I under-stand them to be, of your administration.

I am considering the matter of taking grievance action against you for your lack of support, and for your refusal to investigate the facts that I have presented to you.

c. Grace Maybury

c. Zeb Ramsey

Rick panicked when he read Laurie's memo. It wasn't the content that disturbed him, since he couldn't have cared less what it said, but rather the notation on the bottom, showing that copies had been sent to Grace Maybury and Zeb Ramsey.

He tore from his office and half-walked, half-ran out the nearest Annex exit, across the yard, up the walkway leading to the closest rear entrance to the Main Building, through the doorway, up the stairs to the ground floor, and then down the main corridor to Zeb Ramsey's office. Without knocking, he burst inside, breathlessly, saying that he needed to talk to Zeb right away.

"That's interesting," Zeb responded, "in view of the fact that you've kept yourself so well obscured for so long. How's your ulcer?"

Rick didn't even know how Zeb had learned about his ulcer, but he said, "It's killing me, thanks. But I didn't come here to consult you about my ulcer. I'm here to give my side of the story that you must already have read about, in Laurie Canaday's memo."

He could see the copy on Zeb's desk, on top of a pile of other papers, and it infuriated him just to know that it existed, as if it had a life of its own.

"It's a sick, neurotic attempt to slander me," Rick began. "That nurse has got half the place over there in an uproar with her paranoid ideas, and we could all get along quite well without her.

I've realized for quite some time that her job has been too much for her. I've really seen her change as a person, and she's heading in the same direction that Sharon Lovejoy was taking. I've even tried hard to help her, and I've considered offering her a job in a lesser capacity, but I was afraid that that would destroy her."

He took a deep breath and continued with his running commentary, strings of saliva appearing between his lips. "Anyway, now she's including me in her paranoid delusions, and that's why she's threatening me with filing a grievance against me."

He waited for Zeb to make some response, but Zeb just shook his head.

"I don't know how to handle this, Zeb," Rick said. "She's accusing some of the best people we have at the Annex."

"It looks to me as if you've let this situation get totally out of hand," Zeb said, not offering any help at all but just analyzing Rick's dilemma. "You've let this problem grow from an ant hill into something with major proportions, something that's backfiring in your face. But you need to face it squarely and deal with it. What else can I say? If you don't, it looks as if you're going to have a grievance on your hands. And that's all the advice I have to offer you," he said, the tone of finality in his voice telling Rick that their conversation, though short, was over.

Rick started to speak again, but Zeb shook his head and said, "You've caught me right in the middle of some very important work, so you'll have to leave now." Then he bent his head over some papers, and that was the end of that.

On his way back to his office, Rick pondered his strategy. He really hadn't expected much from that 'weirdo' Ramsey anyway, but he'd hoped that his story about Laurie would cover up what had happened, and that had been his reason for going over there in the first place.

Then he decided to write a memo to Laurie, requesting to meet with her, and to appeal to her to abandon this grievance business, which if pursued, would mean his downfall. He wouldn't, however, tell her that Faith would also be present at the meeting. Maybe Faith could help him to convince Laurie to drop the idea.

"I certainly hope so," he thought, "since otherwise...it means my head is going to roll."

That same afternoon, Rick and Faith, along with Randy Sinclair, had all assembled before Laurie made her entrance into Rick's office, and she was surprised to find so many people present at what she'd thought would be a very private meeting. But Rick began quickly, and trying to start out on the right foot, he said, as Faith had coached him to say, "I'm sorry that you've suddenly chosen to consider filing a grievance, Laurie."

"There was nothing sudden about it," Laurie said. "As you know, it was my last resort after everything else had failed."

"I do understand the tremendous pressure you've been under lately," Rick said, trying to sound compassionate but unable to hide his patronizing tone.

"Yes, it is rather pressing taking the fire from both my subordinates who are demanding action, and my superior, who is refusing to take any," she said, picking up on Rick's usual sarcastic way of answering questions.

"This retaliation wouldn't help you personally, Laurie," Rick said, his tone almost begging. "In fact, people who throw mud very often get it thrown right back into their own faces."

"Are you going to investigate the facts that I've brought to your attention, or not?" she said angrily.

"If I do what you've asked me to do, I would run the risk of destroying the good structure of Unit A which you yourself have put so much effort into," he whined.

"By not dealing with this unethical conduct, and removing these people from my unit, you are destroying it!" she said abruptly.

"When I make rounds on your unit," Faith interrupted, "I never hear anything negative about Doris Pitts."

"That's because my people don't relate to you. They don't trust you. And besides, wasn't it you who criticized Sharon Lovejoy so severely for being afraid to do something about 'that woman'?"

"I find it difficult to believe that Doris Pitts is such a problem, Laurie. In fact, all kinds of people are telling me that you are out to crucify her!"

Laurie started to laugh. "That's very funny, Rick, so I guess I don't have to worry about it."

"You, of all people, know how low the morale is in your unit," Faith said in her hostile voice, and we feel that the low morale and negative feelings are due to your inadequacies in bringing the staff together."

As her eyes pierced into Laurie's, Laurie could see the malice shining through. Even though Faith had advised Rick to try getting into Laurie's confidence by praising her and begging her to forget the grievance idea, she had already lost her cool, seeing that Laurie wasn't about to yield. As Laurie could tell, they hadn't won anything, and weren't about to.

"I know that pursuing a grievance isn't what you really want," Rick said, trying to get her to agree with him.

"What I really want," Laurie said, flippantly, "is to get three people out of my unit, so that my people and I can get on with our work!"

"But transferring problems isn't the answer," Rick insisted. "It's up to you to bring harmony to your unit."

"CAN it, Rick," Laurie said, disgustedly, no longer caring about being a lady, "I'm sick to death of your nauseating rhetoric. Trying to get through to you is like trying to teach a bunch of monkeys how to reason."

"Instead of moving Doris Pitts or Rene Boutelle from your unit," Faith said, her shapeless body tensed like a bow about to release an arrow, "we should think seriously about moving out the Unit Chief!"

Rick and Randy gave Faith a disapproving glance, as she was giving Laurie more ammunition for a grievance proceeding.

"I consider that a threat," Laurie said nonchalantly, as calmly as she could, amused that she had gotten the better of them, "and I don't take kindly to threats."

Finally, Rick couldn't contain himself any longer, and practically shouted at Laurie, "Do you realize that a Governor's Task Force is over in the Main Building RIGHT NOW, investigating conditions at this Institution? The legislators are sick and tired of all the problems here, and one more grievance might result in their closing the place down."

Laurie stood up. She had had enough. But before closing the door behind her, she turned toward them and said, sarcastically, "What does Doris Pitts know that makes her so special? And why is Rene Boutelle helping her to disrupt the smooth functioning of my unit?"

"I want you to get specimens of drainage from all of the skin breaks on this ward," Faith Byrd was saying to Faye Garland, A-2 team leader, "and have them cultured. Then write a report on this series of skin breaks."

"But there are only three skin conditions," Faye said, "and none of them are draining. In two of the cases, Laurie got an order for hydrocortisone cream, and the other is just a heal blister from new shoes which Laurie told us to soak. The other condition is improving, so..."

"So why bother?" Faye wanted to say, "and why bother writing up a report on it?"

"I don't care what Laurie told you to do," Faith said, threateningly. "I'm telling you that I want cultures done on all those areas."

"But there is no drainage," explained Faye.

"Then do skin scrapings," Faith ordered, "and furthermore, I want you to scrub all surfaces of this ward, the adjoining rooms, the beds, and the overhead pipes with sani-phene and green soap. I want all the linen stripped from these beds, marked 'contaminated', and sent to the laundry. And don't forget to make a full written report on all these skin conditions.

"And one more thing," Faith said in conclusion, "If you have any more problems on this ward, you come to me with them." And with those words, she turned and left.

Thinking aloud, Faye said, "I didn't realize I had any problems until she came on the ward," overwhelmed at the prospect of all the cleaning that lay ahead of her.

She paged Dr. Bauer, the Annex physician, to come to the ward to write up the orders for the cultures and the skin scrapings. When he arrived, Faye said to him, "I don't understand the Assistant Administrator. She only trips my ward on Laurie's days off, and why in the world would she want skin scrapings on patients who've had re-occurring psoriasis for years."

"It is quite obvious to me what she is up to," Dr. Bauer said, in his thick middle European accent. "I am aware of Miss Byrd's frequent presence on Miss Canaday's wards on her days off. I will write these orders for these cultures, but the lab will not like it. It will be a lot of unnecessary expense and time for them."

On his way to the Main Building, Dr. Bauer told himself, "This is a terrible thing that is happening. I must speak to Mrs. Maybury about it, before it is too late."

But Grace had been stripped of her power, and as she told him, "I'm here just on an advisory and consultant basis, and no one asks my advice much anymore. Of course, that unhappy state of affairs could all change, depending on what the Governor's Task Force comes up with."

"I have been seeing a lot of strange faces around here lately," the doctor said. "Do you think there will be any changes?"

"The Governor obviously thinks there should be," she said, behaving as though she hadn't expected them.

"You see," continued Dr. Bauer, "I feel as if I were watching a slow murder going on. Isn't there anything you can do to help this girl? I'm afraid she will be eliminated like Mrs. Avery and Miss Lovejoy."

"I'd like to help Laurie," Grace explained, "but in my position, I can't go to her. She must come to me."

"And we can't go to Dr. Ramsey, because Miss Byrd is very close with him. No?"

"Yes," she said. "They're together everyday. Faith leads him around by the nose."

"Then we must go higher," exclaimed Dr. Bauer. "We must contact the State Employees' Association and arrange for a representative to come here and meet with Laurie."

"Try to convince Laurie that taking this action is necessary for her survival at the Annex," Grace said. "Tell her she mustn't let those manipulating bastards drive her out, and then tell her that there is a job waiting for her in the Main Building, any time she wants it."

Laurie didn't realize just how strong her support was, but the next day, she was given one of the most pleasant surprises of her lifetime. While she was tripping the Activity Area, Linda Bryant, A-4 team leader, was just bringing in some of her patients.

"We have put something in writing," she said to Laurie, "and we'd like you to check it over before we send it."

"We?" thought Laurie, wondering who Linda was referring to.

"What is it that you're sending out?" Laurie asked.

"Well, we feel that we must report what's been going on here to someone outside of this Institution."

Betsy Dunn, Activity Director, came over and added, "Faith told me yesterday, that if you move any of the staff, to tell her about it."

"What was that all about?" Laurie asked.

"She only comes in here on your days off, Laurie, asking me if I have any problems," Betsy explained. "Day before yesterday, I just happened to mention that it did get a bit hectic during the busiest morning hours with trying to answer the phone."

"Go on," Laurie urged.

"Faith said that she guessed my Unit Chief wasn't attuned to my problems, and that perhaps she should trip my area. I assured her that you did trip this area every day, and that in fact, you were considering lending me the A-6 ward clerk to help with the phone, just during the peak hours.

"Is there more?" Laurie asked.

"Yesterday, she came stomping in here demanding to know if you had moved any of the staff around. I told her that you hadn't done anything yet, and then she told me that if you did, to tell her about it."

"We never see her," Linda Bryant said, "unless it's on your days off when she comes around looking to make trouble for you, or to visit Rene. She wants you out; that's obvious to everyone around here with a pair of eyes."

"Well," Laurie said, "I can't help you with the wording of the report if it's about me, but I'd certainly be interested to see it."

Linda Bryant passed Laurie a copy of their report, the main thrust of which read:

> *We, the undersigned, are united in the principle of fairness for our Unit Chief, Miss Laurie Canaday, who is being dealt with unfairly by the Annex administration.*
>
> *We see an active attempt to eliminate an excellent nurse whose attempt to do her job has been met with resistance by a small but influential minority. We hope to see a fair conclusion to this problem, and to the administration's unjust way of dealing with its employees.*

Underneath the report, the signers had drawn a large circle, writing their names around it so that no one could tell who had signed first.

As Linda went on to explain, "We're sending copies to the Director of Nurses, to the Superintendent, to the Commissioner, and to the State Employees' Association."

As Laurie read the names, some of which belonged to staff working in Unit B, whose patients had been denied transfer to her unit because of requiring care, she was very much heartened to see that thirty-two individuals cared enough about   proper treatment of the patients and herself, to sign their names in protest to the unethical activity being conducted at the Annex.

CHAPTER NINETEEN

When Sharon Lovejoy called Laurie at work to say she'd just gotten a job at the same general hospital where Laurie had taken her training, Laurie said, "Well, congratulations, Sharon. I'm so happy for you."

"But what about you, Laurie? Are you going to be a permanent resident at Dunton?"

"Right now, I'm smack in the middle of something that scares me a little, Sharon. I was considering filing a grievance against Rick Armstrong, but now I won't have to. My staff wants to file a Class Action grievance against him, and in fact, there's a representative from the State Employees' Association here right now, interviewing everyone. I think Dr. Bauer and Mrs. Maybury sent for him. And do you know what he said to me? He said, 'Your boss has put the word out that you're paranoid and neurotic. So if there really are problems at the Annex, they'll never be resolved if your people don't speak up'."

"Well, I hope for your sake that they do," said Sharon, "but if things don't turn out the way you want, come and see me here, and maybe I can get you back to a place where a nurse is appreciated."

"Well, your people talked, and then some," Stan Simpson of the State Employees' Association reported to Laurie, after interviewing her staff. "I have just been talking with the Commissioner who is here, and we believe that Rick Armstrong, by his failure to deal with a bad situation, allowed it to grow into crisis proportions. Although there were some who were feeding him false information, he should have at least investigated what you were telling him. I'm sure that the action taken against him by the Unit-A staff this afternoon will bring the whole sad story of Rick Armstrong to an end."

"And clear away another obstacle in Faith Byrd's path to the top," exclaimed Joan Decker, passing Stan Simpson on his way out of Laurie's office.

"What do you mean?" asked Laurie. "What's Faith got to do with it?"

"Who do you think is going to replace Rick, once he gets the can tied to his tail?"

"But how could she do that?" Laurie asked. "She's nowhere near qualified for that position."

"That depends on what you mean by 'qualified'," said Joan. "Her lover will just slide her into that position."

"Her lover?" Laurie said. "You mean Zeb Ramsey?"

Joan threw her head back and laughed. "You're incredible Laurie! You're just...too naive for words. And I guess Rick Armstrong was naive too. He'll probably never know that she set him up. <u>She</u> brought him to the edge, Laurie. <u>You</u> pushed him over."

"Maybury said we could sign a petition against Faith's appointment as Annex administrator, but doubted it would do any good, since she has Zeb all signed and sealed, just sitting comfortably in her pocket."

And of course, Joan was correct. Faith could now brag and boast that she had so far successfully eliminated a Unit Chief, a Director of Nurses, and an Administrator, replacing each one in turn in her ruthless climb to the top.

When Zeb Ramsey announced that he had appointed Faith Byrd to the top Annex administrative post, no one was particularly surprised, since they had expected it. But their predicting the event didn't make it any easier for them to swallow. The nurses were furious, and commiserated with each other.

"I'm disgusted," Nurse Kathryn Scott, new A-8 team leader said. Even though a registered nurse, Kathryn had been hired as team leader, to take charge of that very difficult ward.

"Grace Maybury told us it wouldn't do a bit of good to send a petition around, but I hate to admit she was right. I haven't been here very long, but I've already had it up to my neck, and I'm leaving. But believe me, I intend to make my feelings known to Zeb Ramsey before I go."

"I'm putting in my notice too," Joan Decker said, "and I'm going to give Ramsey a piece of my mind before I leave."

"I guess I might as well go along with you," Laurie said, despairingly. "I don't think my chances of survival here are very good."

"Leave only when you're damn good and ready," Joan advised her. "Don't let her drive you out. You have more at stake here than we do, since we're just newcomers. The only way you can beat her is at her own game. And it would only make things worse for you if you were to talk to Zeb Ramsey now. She's taken care of that by convincing him that you're paranoid, so he'd only attribute everything you said to your paranoia. It would be much better for you to just keep your mouth shut."

As the days went on, and the nurses were working out their last weeks, Faith tried to get them to stay on, realizing the implications of their leaving, and Laurie was worried that they would give in to her compliments and just leave silently. Kathryn kept telling her, "Faith corrals me every day, begging me to stay! She says she can't bear to lose me, and has even offered to let me work any hours that I want, in any capacity that I want, to keep me here."

"I really don't think Faith has the authority to make such an offer," Laurie kept telling her.

Even though Laurie could now see Faith's manipulative wheels rolling, she knew that Kathryn was falling for her grandstand play, to stop her from unloading to Zeb Ramsey, as she had vowed to do.

Faith even went so far as to circulate a memo stating that Joan Decker and Kathryn Scott were the two best nurses that Dunton had ever seen, and she didn't know how she was ever going to get along without them.

"Well, that takes care of both of them," Laurie thought, after reading the memo. "I'm sure neither of them will feel like speaking up about Faith after this sleazy maneuver!"

And she was right. Neither Kathryn nor Joan said anything to Zeb Ramsey when they left, leaving Laurie out on a limb, their silence bought with a few words of cheap flattery.

"And they saw through her before I did," she thought to herself, after they left. "They even warned me against her."

It took a tremendous emotional effort to get through each day now, but Laurie couldn't see into the future, and had to take each day as it came, to conserve her strength. She was losing weight and her face grew paler every day.

"If this is how Sharon felt, then I'm only beginning to understand why she had to leave," she thought.

One afternoon, as she was tripping A-2, Faye Garland told her the news that they were going to start implementing Behavior Modification at the Annex, now that Rick was gone.

"Ramsey's written an application for a grant," she said, "and if it's approved, and they think it most certainly will be, then we'll have to start modifying our patients' behaviors the way they've been doing in the Main Building."

"And how did you find this out?" Laurie said, curious that she didn't seem to be on the same grapevine as the aides.

"Faith told us," Faye said. "She's already sent Rene over to Zeb's unit in the Main Building to learn how to be a 'facilitator'."

"What in the world is a 'facilitator'?" Laurie said.

"That's a tutor in the Behavior Modification techniques. When she's trained, she'll be coming back over to teach all the rest of us."

"That sounds cozy," Laurie said. "It would have been nice, and more proper, if Faith had consulted me as to her choice of a 'facilitator', or at least informed me of what she was doing. After all, it is my unit that's involved!"

"But I can't expect any consideration from Faith," she thought, "not even the common courtesy of telling me what she's up to."

Laurie had many misgivings about Behavior Modification. She remembered Sharon's experience, and she had not been unaware of the many scandalous reports about that program.

CHAPTER TWENTY

When the Governor's Task Force published its findings, it was decided that Dr. Shada's Skilled-Care Unit was an unfair financial burden on the taxpayers. Since the unit was never filled to capacity, was never in fact even half-filled, the report indicated that it would be more feasible to send sick patients to the Medical Center. Therefore, Dr. Shada and his unit were terminated.

The PERU team was declared to be of no particular benefit to the patients, and therefore not financially justifiable.

Mrs. Strenge's position was found to be superfluous, and it was eliminated.

The activity attendant who was fired for insubordination, because he questioned Mrs. Strenge's many absences from the Institution, was reinstated.

Nathan Strenge's departure soon followed, putting an end to 'unitization'. Strenge had been on thin ice ever since he approved leave for sex killer Terrance Long.

Centralization was re-established, and Grace Maybury was reinstated as Director of Nursing. Zeb Ramsey moved up into Dunton's highest administrative post.

On Zeb's Behavior Modification Unit in the Main Building, sixty-four-year-old patient Della Frazier wasn't performing her assigned task of washing the floor. It wasn't clear whether she was deliberately disobeying the order, whether she just didn't feel like it, or even if she understood the order in the first place.

Attendant Aaron Broderick grabbed her hand, and held it onto the mop, forcing her to mop the floor.

"You crazy old fool!" he shouted. "You mop this floor as you've been assigned to do."

Della may have been old, but she was still sane enough to be offended by his remarks and by his pushing her around. So she gave him her elbow, and then turned, facing him. When she raised her hand as if to strike him, he crouched down low, picked her up, and tossed her over his shoulder, which caused her to land on the floor, taking the blow to her left leg. And there she lay, without moving.

"You've probably gone a little too far this time," said Zeb Ramsey who happened to enter the ward just in time to make him a witness to the incident.

Rene Boutelle, in the process of training to be a 'facilitator', ran over to help Aaron drag Della to a chair. But Della couldn't sit up straight; she kept slumping forward, as if she were about to fall out of the chair.

"You'd better put her to bed," Zeb advised them. "I don't think we need to mention this to anyone. We'll tell people that she doesn't feel well and is remaining in bed for a couple of days."

He didn't even lower his voice or try to couch his opinions in vague terms. And as Rene pulled the covers up to Della's chin, Zeb continued. "I'm afraid that one more incident on this unit would result in the termination of our Program, and consequently our funding. People around here, especially these nurses, don't seem to appreciate the benefits derived from our program.

He had apparently given this little speech many times before, since he droned on and on in his monotone voice, as if he hated having to repeat anything that was so obvious to him.

"I don't think we all want to be out of a job, do we? Also, I don't want my application for a grant for the Annex jeopardized, and it most certainly would be if there were any more incidents over here."

Patients Millie Walker and Rose Atkins who had seen what occurred, were standing so stock-still, they looked like statues.

"Don't worry about them," Zeb said, brushing his hand through the air as if he were brushing them off. "No one would pay any attention to them. They're hardly competent enough to tell you their own names or what year it is."

And so when the next shift arrived to take over, Aaron informed them that Della didn't feel good, and should probably just remain in bed.

Early the next morning, about five-thirty, eleven-to-seven aide Sarah Archer noticed that Della's position was exactly the same as it was when Sarah had come on duty at eleven-o'clock the evening before. Also, Sarah noticed that Della was lying without moving a muscle and was not asleep. Sarah leaned down and said, "What's the matter, Della? Why aren't you asleep?"

"Because it hurts," Della said.

"What hurts?" Sarah asked.

"It hurts to move, to breathe too deeply," Della said.

Sarah investigated Della's "hurt", and found half of her left buttock and outer left thigh to be reddened and swollen, and very hot to her touch. Because Della had been unable to ambulate to the bathroom, she had soiled her bed. Sarah was repulsed by the presence of fecal material in Della's large, open wound.

"How in the world did this happen?" Sarah asked.

"A man picked me up and threw me over his shoulder," Della said. "I landed on the floor, and that's when it started hurting. I think maybe he broke something inside."

"Jesus Christ!" Sarah muttered, running to call Dr. Mezummi, the duty doctor, to the ward.

When he arrived, Dr. Mezummi examined the patient, and in a shocked voice said, "This patient has a compound leg fracture complicated by an infection! Why wasn't this reported sooner? What in the world is going on here?"

When Sarah had no response, the doctor asked her if there was anything on Della's chart about an injury.

"No," she said. "And there was no mention of anything like that happening in the report either. I was simply told that she did not want supper and was remaining in bed because she didn't feel very good."

"Well, get her records together," he ordered, "we're sending her to the hospital immediately. For God's sake, how could something like this happen, with no one knowing anything about it?"

As the day-shift staff arrived, Dr. Mezummi told them that during the night, Della Frazier had been found to have a broken leg.

"Does anyone know anything about it?" he asked. Looking from face to face, the doctor saw only surprise and ignorance. But finally one of the aides said, "I just was told that Della didn't feel well, and was spending a couple of days in bed."

"Della did trip and fall over me yesterday," Aaron Broderick said, "but I didn't think anything of it at the time."

"Oh, that's right," Rene said, as if she'd suddenly remembered the incident. "I saw it happen, but it was nothing, really, doctor!"

"Was anyone else around?"

"No, it was just the two of us," Rene said.

The doctor was obviously frustrated, shaking his head and fanning the air with his upturned hands.

"But hasn't anyone even looked at this patient? Hasn't anyone been caring for her? If you had, you would have noticed that large, open wound."

"But we thought she was just lying in bed because she didn't feel good," one of the aides said. "There was nothing to notice or recognize; I just thought she was sound asleep because she wasn't moving."

"Apparently she hadn't moved at all, after she fell down, because it gave her too much pain," said Dr. Mezummi. "It's just too bad her injury went unnoticed for so long, because now it has been complicated by an infection, and also, her surgery surely won't be as successful as it would have been had it been performed immediately after the fracture was sustained." Then the doctor turned in a huff, and was gone.

As the staff discussed the incident among themselves, Sarah Archer who had discovered Della's injury was thinking, "But she didn't say she had fallen down. She said, 'A man threw me over his shoulder, and I landed on the floor'."

And those were the exact words she used in her report of the incident which she submitted to Grace Maybury.

When Grace Maybury received and read Sarah's report, she slammed it down on her desk and shouted, "I'm sick to death at the lack of action on my reports about what's been going on in that unit! I'm writing a letter to the Commissioner, washing my hands of the whole mess."

Never in her wildest dreams had she imagined that she and a handful of others would end up testifying before a Grand Jury about the affair. After receiving Maybury's letter, the Department of Mental Health and Corrections conducted an investigation which resulted in a Grand Jury hearing.

When Aaron was called to testify on his own behalf, he stuck to his guns, perpetuating the falsehood that Della had tripped and fallen over him. Rene backed him up, fully supporting his story

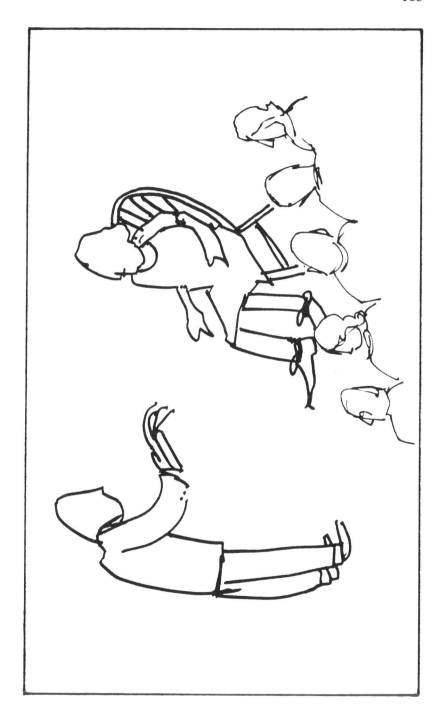

and never revealing that Zeb Ramsey had also seen the "accident" and suggested that they cover it up.

The two patients who had also seen Aaron pick up Della and throw her down were called as witnesses, but they hardly seemed to know what was going on, or what was really expected of them, and had a great deal of trouble speaking about the event without mentioning many unrelated details about their inner lives, their fears and nightmares.

Even the hardened Rene Boutelle felt a twinge of guilt when the patients told their stories, and were then make fools of by Aaron's attorney. Poor Rose Atkins was so nervous and fearful that she told the prosecutor that she really liked him. This naively-given compliment seemed to have the opposite effect, turning the prosecutor against her, since he nodded in sympathy, but looked as if he wanted her removed from the witness stand as quickly as possible. When he said she could step down, she didn't understand at first. And when he loudly repeated that she should step down, she suddenly darted out of the seat, and then caused a commotion by attempting to escape.

Two attendants rushed up to stop her from running away. It was then concluded that both patients' testimonies should be disregarded, since they were obviously incompetent, due to the extreme severity of their mental illnesses.

But Della's abuse was only the first in a long list of accusations of mistreatment brought to light, and when it became known that similar abuses were committed and even encouraged in this unit every day, it was determined that it would have been unfair to single out Aaron as a scapegoat. So Aaron was not indicted, but the program itself was. It was ordered terminated by the Department of Mental Health.

Zeb's three-hundred-thousand-dollar grant application to institute Behavior Modification at the Annex was approved, and Rene Boutelle returned as its 'facilitator'.

One morning Laurie came to work to find that her wards were practically deserted of staff.

"Where is everybody?" she asked an aide on A-5.

"Potter's at the meeting, Laurie," the aide said.

"And what meeting is that?" Laurie asked. "I didn't hear about any meeting."

"Faith and Rene have been telling all the available staff to attend the first meeting on setting up the new Behavior Modification program on this unit. Rene's back and I guess she's going to be in charge of it," the aide said.

"That's interesting," Laurie declared sharply, wondering what effect this would have on her position.

There were more and more meetings, but Laurie was not informed. Her people kept her well-posted and up-to-date, but no one ever consulted her for her advice. She had no input anymore, and wondered what purpose she now served, since she was being left out of the happenings on her unit.

And then came the memo to all the staff from Faith:

> *As you have probably all heard, Dr. Ramsey's application for a Behavior Modification grant for Unit A has been approved. In keeping with this focus, the new position facilitator of Behavior Modification Techniques' will be appropriately replacing the Unit-A Chief position.*

"Will be appropriately replacing?" Laurie said out loud, after reading that her own position had been eliminated. "Where does that leave me now?" she thought, reading on.

> *As you may also know, Rene Boutelle has recently completed a course on Dr. Ramsey's Behavior Modification unit in the Main Building, and is now an authority on the appropriate techniques. For this reason, I have appointed*

*her to this position. Her duties will be to set up
and coordinate this method of treatment on Unit A,
and I am sure that you will all give her your full
cooperation.*

Laurie felt more relief than anything else. Her decision to stay or not to stay had been made for her. She suddenly remembered Sharon's warning, "She'll get you out too." On an impulse, she went straight to the Main Building to the personnel office and submitted her resignation.

CHAPTER TWENTY- ONE

Grace Maybury asked Laurie to meet her in the employees' locker room in the Annex basement so that Faith wouldn't see them.

"I hate having to sneak around this way," Maybury said, looking over her shoulder, "and of course it doesn't matter to you anymore, since you're leaving. But I need to hang on here a few more years for my pension. And believe me, I don't know if I'll be able to stay here long enough to collect it!"

"But I didn't ask you down here to talk about me. I wanted to tell you, Laurie, that I've never gotten so much feedback in all the years that I've been here, as I've gotten on your resignation. Two doctors approached my desk this morning to ask me if there was anything I could do to keep you here. I told them a job was open and waiting for you in the Main Building.

"And now I'm telling you. I'll hold it for three months if you want to take some time off to help you get over this terrible ordeal. You've been a helluva good nurse, and I hate to see you being shafted. It's criminal what's been done to you, and you deserve a leave of absence."

"I appreciate it very much," Laurie said, "but it's time for me to go. I couldn't possibly remain here with people like that. I would like to tell Zeb Ramsey a thing or to before I go."

"I wouldn't do that if I were you," Maybury said. "She's got him wrapped around her little finger, as if you didn't already know. You'd just be hurting yourself. Joan Decker and Kathryn Scott never mentioned anything to him after swearing that they were going to. Did you see the beautiful memo she wrote about them?"

"Oh, yes," Laurie said. "Of course. And I guess it would be pretty hard to convince Ramsey on my own that Faith is such an unscrupulous manipulator, after she said that Joan and Kathryn were the two best nurses who ever came down the pike. She made all sorts of offers to Kathryn too; told her she could work however, wherever, and whenever she chose, if only she would stay."

"And you know very well that she couldn't have done that," Maybury said.

"That's what I told Kathryn, but it didn't make any difference. She yielded to the flattery."

"Do you know that on account of their remaining silent, Faith came out of this whole mess smellin' like a rose in Ramsey's eyes? It was really an amazing bit of workmanship, if you think of it. And you've got to give the woman some credit for being the most conniving, evil witch who's ever slithered on this earth. I tried to tell Zeb Ramsey what she was up to, but he wouldn't hear me. He wouldn't even listen."

"And she used me to get rid of Rick for her," Laurie said. "He might have been a 'do-nothing', but she's deadly."

"Please reconsider leaving, and come over to work in the Main Building," Maybury said. "If you do transfer over, your position will be transferred permanently with you, so that whenever you did decide to leave, your position would remain in the Main Building."

Laurie shook her head and said, "Thanks for the offer, anyway. But I can't work in this establishment anymore. I guess my days here were numbered to begin with, but I didn't want to see it. I didn't want to face the ugly facts. Now my rose-colored glasses are off, and all I can see is ugliness in poisonous black and white!"

"You know," Maybury said, taking Laurie's arm and walking out the door with her, "Faith is after my job now. She's already squeezed me off two of my committees."

Although neither Laurie nor Maybury were aware of it, their conversation had been overheard by the head of the Annex Housekeeping Department, Orman Hobbs. Not wanting to miss an opportunity to make some points with his boss, Orman went directly to Faith Byrd's office after waiting in silence behind a partially-closed door for both Laurie and Maybury to leave.

"Yes?" Faith asked archly, when Orman tapped on her door.

"Miss Byrd, I just heard something I thought you might be interested in hearing."

"Really?" she asked wearily, not particularly eager to hear him. However, once he began, her weariness disappeared.

For his part, Orman expressed the conversation as dramatically as he was able, knowing that passing on the information could earn him some real points with Faith Byrd.

"Thank you, Orman," she said when he'd concluded his story. "This is really quite interesting -- quite interesting indeed."

He nodded and backed out of her office, knowing that he had improved his standing in his boss's eyes.

Alone again in her office, Faith stood up and faced the window, considering the significance of what she had learned.

"So, Maybury thinks she can hang on, does she?" she thought, chuckling to herself. The idea that Maybury retained any power in the Institution was comical. No, Faith wasn't concerned about that. However, she did need to get her out, and she knew exactly how she was going to proceed.

Faith had not missed the talk that Doris Pitts had "something on the higher-ups", nor had she been unaware of the preferential treatment enjoyed by Doris over the years, and still being enjoyed.

"Yes, she murmured to herself, "I think it's time to apply the pressure on Grace Maybury."

Meanwhile, Laurie left the building quietly. She didn't want a farewell celebration. She felt no joy upon leaving. Her experience at Dunton Institution had marked a terrifying journey for her -- one in which she not only felt her own innocence and idealism give way, but one in which she recognized the cruelty and evil of power-hungry people.

Her staff shared her sadness upon leaving. Each understood perfectly Laurie's need and desire to slip from the Institution like a wraith or a shadow. Each understood the pain that she took with her as she left.

As she drove away, careful not to look back, she considered what she would do next. She knew that she would need time to restore something of her faith in herself and in human nature. Even the pain of seeing Perley day by day inch toward the abyss hadn't damaged her so much as the evil to which she had been witness.

She tried concentrating her thoughts on good people such as Mother Theresa and the nuns who had once inspired her. Those thoughts seemed to fill her with hope, and she pressed down harder on the accelerator, speeding away from Dunton and an experience that would color the rest of her life.

PART III

REVENGE FROM THE GRAVE

CHAPTER TWENTY-TWO

Tara Doyle had often replayed in her mind the phone call she'd gotten from Dunton informing her that her mother had "taken a dramatic turn for the worse." She could clearly hear the doctor's hushed voice telling her that her mother had had another "episode". She remembered the frantic drive to the Institution wondering if her mother would still be alive when she got there, and how her father could not bear to go inside, expecting the worst.

Tara's relationship with her mother was a complicated one. They had gotten along wonderfully during Tara's young years. Then, Virgie's epileptic fits were few and very far between. Although not completely controlled by medication, they didn't begin until Tara was five, and except for the terror of a convulsion itself, didn't really disrupt their lives.

Then, Virgie was a kind woman with a fondness for baking. Tara could still remember the oatmeal cookies her mother used to bake. The epilepsy convinced Virgie and her husband not to have any more children. Their doctor had warned that the epilepsy could be passed along or that a seizure at the wrong time could even damage the fetus in utero.

"We just don't know enough about it," he confessed to them. "Why take unnecessary chances?"

So, in spite of her own wishes for a brother or a sister, Tara remained an only child. Her father was older than Virgie, and worked long hours in an insurance firm. In addition, he was a distant man who had trouble showing his emotions.

Tara's passion and love of life came from her mother. However, that joyfulness changed dramatically after her mother's accident. Virgie had been crossing four lanes of traffic on her way to the grocery store. Three lanes stopped to let her pass. The driver in the fourth never even saw her, never slowed down. Both her legs were broken. Her skull was fractured.

Tara knew something was terribly wrong when her father was at the house to greet her when she returned home from school.

"Where's Mom?" she asked.

He lowered his eyes.

"Where's Mom?" she demanded, stamping her feet.

"Your mother was hurt," he said softly, not looking at her. "She was hit by a car and hurt very badly."

"Is she...?" Tara couldn't form the word "dead" because what had been a strange and frightening concept suddenly seemed immediate and real.

"No, no, no," her father said quickly. "The doctors say she'll be all right...it'll take a while though. And...and she won't be the same."

It was a month before Tara was able to visit her mother at the hospital, and even then she couldn't believe how bad her mother looked. Her face was still swollen and the bruises were still evident. Her legs were in casts, but the fact was, they were going to be useless to her.

Three months later, Virgie was discharged from the hospital. However, she wasn't able to go home. No, she couldn't function at home. Her disabilities had become too pronounced. In addition, the head injury which she sustained seemed to have aggravated her epilepsy. She had more seizures during her four months in the hospital than she'd had in the previous six years.

"I can't have her at home," Tara's father said to Dr. Bahai, Dunton's Assistant Superintendent. "I have a young daughter. It's too much."

While Virgie was institutionalized, Tara was brought up by her father's mother -- a bright, if less than cheerful woman.

When she entered her early teenage years, Tara hated her mother. She hated her for being what she was, for having gotten into an accident, and for having to live in that cold, horrible Institution.

By the time she was fourteen, Tara, having had to grow up faster than most other girls, stopped hating her mother and resenting her visits to her.

It was only during those visits, when Tara was with her, that Virgie was able to drop the manipulative persona that she had taken on in the Institution, and showed traces of the kind woman she'd once been. Virgie used to confide in Tara the dealings at Dunton.

"It's horrible how they treat these patients," Virgie told her. "They treat them like animals. My Lord, it seems they care more about keeping the floor clean than they do about these poor people. Can you imagine?"

Tara couldn't imagine, and in fact sometimes thought her mother must be exaggerating. Even when her mother described the nurse whom she had caught swapping narcotic capsules for others in her purse -- who could never transfer off the ward or Virgie would tell on her -- Tara wasn't sure.

"Mother, how can you say that?" she would ask, certain it couldn't be true.

"You don't believe me?" Virgie would ask, surprised. "I can prove it," she said. "Just watch how this nurse lets me do whatever I please. That should convince you."

Although it did seem that Grace Maybury allowed Virgie to "wrap her around her little finger", she did it with a clever, condescending smile, making it seem that she was only humoring Virgie. Tara noted that smile, realizing that it was possible that her mother was sicker than she truly understood.

By this time, Tara was in high school, and very precocious. She had come to understand how difficult life had been for her mother all these years. She had come full circle -- from hating Virgie for her disability to respecting her for how she managed to survive in spite of it.

After Virgie died, Tara began to recall a great many things that her mother had told her -- things that she'd tended to dismiss at the time, like Virgie's claim that her Dilatin capsules hadn't felt as firm against her tongue as they usually did.

This revelation had come just three days before she died, at Tara's last visit.

"Come on, Mother," Tara had said. "Even your tongue can't be that sensitive."

"It's true," Virgie said. "I'll bet that nurse is pricking them with a needle and removing the medication..."

"Mother!" Tara had said in alarm. "Don't talk like that. I swear, I think this place has made you paranoid too."

At that, Virgie eyed her daughter. "Even paranoids have real enemies, dear."

Tara had never forgotten about that exchange, nor about the fact that the nurse whom her mother had claimed could never leave her ward or she would expose her, did in fact leave the ward immediately following her mother's death, to become the Director of Nursing.

In the ten years since her mother's death, she had been haunted with many suspicions -- suspicions that she secretly hoped she could someday confirm. In her memory, Dunton had become even more sinister than it had appeared to her as a child and teenager.

In fact, there was a point in her college education, when she was reading Dante's Inferno, when she was convinced that upon reaching the inner ring of hell, she would find Dunton there.

CHAPTER TWENTY-THREE

"This marks the end of many years of waiting and planning," Tara Doyle told herself as she drove the final mile toward Dunton.

She glanced at herself in the rearview mirror -- a pretty young woman with dark hair and dark, intelligent eyes. A certified psychologist, she was twenty-five years old now, no longer the girl whose many visits to Dunton had made it such an integral part of her life. Like her mother, she was, in many ways, a creature of an institution. This sensitivity made her aware from her very first steps inside the Main Building that something was very wrong here.

Tara's arrival evoked many strange feelings for her. There was, of course, the memory of her last visit to see her mother alive, and the many layers of visits before that. In addition, there was the memory of her very last visit to the Institution -- to the morgue -- to kiss her mother good-bye.

"Ah, Ms. Doyle," Zeb Ramsey said, coming down the hallway to greet Tara, shortly after she announced her arrival at the switchboard. "So nice to see you."

Tara looked at Zeb's face, his long beard beginning to turn gray, and smiled. "Hello, Dr. Ramsey..."

"Oh, please, call me Zeb," he insisted. He moved his hands, indicating that she should follow him to his office. "This way."

Tara followed him down the hallway to his office. Although there were bright, cheerful paintings on the walls -- a recent addition -- she found the place much more drab than when she'd last seen it.

"Please, come in," Zeb said, opening his office door for Tara. "Ms. Doyle..."

"Tara," she said quickly.

Zeb smiled. "Of course. Tara, I'd like you to meet the administrator of the Annex, Faith Byrd. Faith, this is Tara Doyle. Tara is a psychologist and is applying for a position at our Institution."

Tara turned her attention to the other person in the room. She was immediately uncomfortable under the penetrating scrutiny of this mannish woman with a cold look in her eyes. She felt as if she were being undressed and examined in the most callous manner. Still, Tara managed to rise above that.

"How do you do, Ms. Byrd?"

"Nice to meet you, Ms. Doyle." Faith accepted Tara's extended hand. As she held it, she marveled at its softness and that of her silky, dark hair, and was filled with desire for this pretty young woman.

"Why don't we have a seat?" Zeb said, smiling nervously at both women.

"Thank you," Tara said.

Faith simply sat down, not acknowledging Zeb for a moment. She leaned forward in her chair and addressed Tara.

"It would be a pleasure to have you join us over at the Annex," she began.

Tara turned to Zeb. "I'm not familiar with the Annex," she said.

He waved aside her ignorance. "Don't worry, I'll explain everything to you,"

But Faith continued as though this brief exchange never happened. "We really need a competent psychologist in the Annex. I'd like to replace our current foul-mouthed, do-nothing psychologist. His presence has created nothing but dissension among the staff..."

Tara looked away. She wasn't comfortable hearing another person so bluntly criticized. What she didn't realize was that this "foul-mouthed, do-nothing psychologist" was already on his way out.

A moment later, Tara looked back at Faith. "That's a very kind invitation," she said, smiling briefly.

"However, at least for now, I'd prefer to remain in the Main Building working on the 'female side'."

"Of course," Faith said coldly, acknowledging the rebuff as gracefully as she could, which was to say not very gracefully at all. Still, she could find nothing offensive about Tara's declining the invitation.

What she didn't know was the special reason for Tara's wanting to work on the female side. She had within her the beginnings of a "mission". She was determined to satisfy herself once and for all about the circumstances of her mother's death, and there was no better place to do that than from the same ward where her mother had been a patient.

"I think that's an appropriate choice," Zeb Ramsey was saying. "Behavior Modification is the preferred method of treatment at this Institution."

"Of course," Tara said quickly.

"We know we have your total commitment to our program," Zeb said. "You see, we have already received grant money to institute it at the Annex..."

"Why did you begin the program at the Annex, rather than over here?" Tara asked.

"Ah," Zeb sighed. "Actually, we did begin here in the Main Building, but a glitch appeared in our grant application, forcing a slight moratorium in the program. We are very hopeful of implementing Behavior Modification throughout the entire Institution."

Tara nodded her head.

"Now we will be expecting you to design and help implement patient treatment plans -- based on sound Behavior Modification techniques, of course -- as basic to your responsibilities on the treatment team. Additionally, you will be responsible for monitoring the progress of these plans, as well as evaluating patients and recommending them for discharge."

"As I'm sure you're aware, deinstitutionalization is the name of the game these days. It's as much the result of economics as it is philosophical or psychological. There simply are not the resources to house these patients indefinitely."

He smiled. "Why, when I first came here, I think the nurses' primary orientation was to hold onto patients for their own emotional needs -- like mothers unwilling to relinquish their children to adulthood.

"Now, we have found the teaching of responsibility to be particularly successful in preparing our patients for life outside the Institution. However, our program has not been as successful as it should have been."

"Why is that?" Tara asked.

"Primarily it is due to dependency-creating nurses who believe in coddling the patients," he said.

To this, Faith nodded her head in satisfaction.

"In any case," Zeb was concluding, "We welcome you to our staff. I think you'll find your work here quite rewarding."

"Yes," Tara said, "I'm sure I will."

CHAPTER TWENTY- FOUR

Tara began her work on the 'female side' as she had requested, starting on her mother's old ward. She called the staff together and introduced herself to them.

"I know the unique challenge that faces all of you every day," Tara said. "However, I'm going to ask of you nothing less than what I expect of myself -- that we help to bring some quality to the lives of our patients."

"When possible, we will prepare them for life outside this Institution. When that is not possible, we will treat them with the same dignity that every human being requires and deserves."

The staff was impressed by what Tara was saying, although there remained a strong current of skepticism.

"Oh yeah," one aide whispered to another, "it's easy to talk. Let's see if she puts her money where her mouth is."

They saw quickly. Tara was determined to be anything but a "pencil pusher". She wanted to be on the front lines in the battle for decent treatment for the mentally ill. She took an active role in every aspect of her patients' care. She also took an obvious interest in her staff -- a genuine one that helped the staff respond to her.

Tara organized group and individual therapy sessions. She facilitated activities that were designed to help her patients come out of their shells. She encouraged input from her staff to help determine the best course of treatment for individual patients, after studying their old records to learn everything she could about their backgrounds.

The staff was amazed at her tenacity and dedication to her patients.

As Tara worked her mother's old ward, she saw that precious little had changed in ten years. Even the physical environment was unchanged. Curtainless, barred windows remained. Zombie-like creatures inhabited the cold, empty hallway, each living a private hell.

As she walked the hall, Tara saw some familiar faces -- older and more worn, but familiar. Whenever she saw a pair of eyes that she recognized, she became deeply saddened -- bombarded with memories of her many visits to her mother. It was at those times that she realized how much a part of her the Institution was -- how interwoven these sights and smells were with her life on the outside, where people were sane and healthy.

Seeing these patients, Tara was always reminded of how desperately she had wanted to help them, to ease some of their overwhelming burden. That was, after all, the reason she had gone into psychology; one of the reasons she had returned to Dunton.

On her third day, Tara's eyes fell upon a familiar face -- a face that caused her to take a deep breath and balance herself. Ellie Matheson was now old enough to be considered an adult, yet her face remained that of a child -- a sad and troubled child.

Of course Tara recognized her immediately. Ellie's face had been etched into her memory, not only by her seeing it when she had visited her mother, but by what her mother had told her about Ellie's life at Dunton.

"You see her?" Virgie had said to her daughter, nodding her head in Ellie's direction. "One of the psychologists is satisfying his lust at her expense. Poor girl. I don't know how much she even understands."

Tara looked at Ellie when her mother had told her about her, and had felt a deep tremor run through her. After all, they were almost the same ages. Why should poor Ellie have been subjected to such abuse?

"Can't anyone do anything about it?" Tara had asked.

Virgie shrugged. "Who's gonna do anything? No one believes us patients, and her family almost never visits. They don't care about her at all."

"But you know what's going on. You could tell someone," Tara insisted.

But Virgie shook her head. Although she knew she could report the incidents, she also knew that she had more power by withholding the information and using it to get as many favors as possible. Blackmail was more profitable than ethics.

As she looked at the older Ellie, Tara felt again the anger and frustration she'd felt over ten years earlier when her mother had told her about Ellie. "And helpless," she thought to herself. "It was the helplessness that was the most horrible."

Tara wondered if maybe that wasn't what hurt the patients the most -- the all-consuming helplessness of their lives. They didn't have control over the most basic facets of their lives. Without some control, how could they have any dignity? Any humanity?

She looked at Ellie and wondered if, even at this late date, there was anything she could do to make it up to her, to somehow give her back some of her life.

What Tara didn't know was that Ellie was a silent witness to her mother's death and the key to the puzzle she'd been trying to piece together for over ten years.

CHAPTER TWENTY- FIVE

Tara worked closely with Ellie, patiently interviewing her and getting to know her. Throughout the interviews, in which she learned of Ellie's parents' rejection of their daughter, she listened caringly. Her emotions were so clear to Ellie that, in a burst of trust and love, she blurted out to Tara, "Will you be my sister?"

Tara smiled and let her pencil rest on the yellow pad she was holding. "Ellie, there's nothing I would like more in this world," she said sincerely.

Ellie smiled broadly as grateful tears filled her eyes.

It was during one of her informal interviews with Ellie that Tara first met Randy Sinclair. As the two women were talking, Randy entered the ward and came directly toward them.

"Ellie," he said in a quiet, firm manner, "it's time for your treatment."

Ellie cowered from him. Tara noted her reaction, but more, she recognized the peculiarity of the situation. "Who are you?" she asked him directly.

"I'm Randy Sinclair, psychologist from the Annex," he said brusquely. "I regularly work with Ellie."

Randy, whose attention had been on Ellie, silently willing her to her room, turned to Tara and said, "And who the hell are you?" in his own special way.

Tara stood up and faced Randy. "I am the new psychologist assigned to this unit," she answered, "and Ellie is my patient now."

Randy backed down. "Sorry," he mumbled. "Anyway," he went on, "I've been treating Ellie for a number of years now. Even though I was transferred to the Annex, I've continued to work with her."

"That's very noble of you," Tara said. "However, Ellie is my patient now." She held Ellie's chart firmly in her hands. "I would appreciate your briefing me on your treatment approach. Because, Mr. Sinclair, I don't see very many comments by you in her record."

"Jesus Christ," he muttered under his breath. "I don't know what happened to the documentation," he stammered. Then he reluctantly exited the ward.

Once he was gone, Tara turned toward Ellie's room, finding the young patient sitting stiffly on the edge of her bed. When Ellie saw that it was Tara, she relaxed noticeably.

"Ellie? Are you all right?"

Ellie nodded slightly.

"Mr. Sinclair will not be seeing you today, Ellie," Tara said quietly.

Ellie's eyes filled with tears.

"It's all right, Ellie," Tara went on. "I'm going to try to take over your care myself. Okay?"

Ellie, who couldn't speak for the emotion filling her throat, nodded.

After she left Ellie's room, the incident remained with Tara, troubling her greatly. It was clear that something was terribly wrong -- but what?

When she had her regular meeting with her staff later in the day, Tara raised the subject. "What is the situation with Randy Sinclair and Ellie?" she asked directly, as was her manner.

"He's been treating her on a regular basis for many years," she was told, "even after he was transferred to the Annex."

"Why is there no documentation of this in Ellie's chart?" Tara asked.

This question was met with silence.

"We're just aides," one of them said, finally. "We can't question the doctors or the psychologists."

"And why would he single out Ellie for treatment? Didn't you ever find it strange that he would single her out for such a long course of treatment?"

Again, the response was that aides did not question their superiors. "Besides," one of them said, "Mrs. Maybury knows he still treats Ellie, and she doesn't question it. Randy has been treating Ellie ever since she was the nurse in charge of this ward."

Tara was overwhelmed by what she was hearing. She did learn that the aides were uncomfortable with what seemed to be happening, that the sessions always took place behind closed doors, and that Ellie always kept to herself for a long time after each 'treatment'.

"Didn't that strike you as being odd?" Tara asked, challenging her staff. "Lord, it certainly couldn't have made these treatments seem very beneficial to you, could it?

"Ellie's record doesn't show any documentation of these sessions, nor are there any progress notes on her chart. Didn't that ever strike you as a little odd?"

Again, they repeated, "We're just aides."

However, in spite of her frustration, Tara knew everything she needed to know. She knew that Randy was the psychologist who had used Ellie to satisfy his lust. With that knowledge, she knew that she had finally found an avenue to pursue her mission. Ellie would be her helper. And, in the process, she would help Ellie get better.

"I just want you to know," she concluded to her staff, "that just because you're aides, I don't expect you to disengage your minds or your hearts. If something strikes you as being odd, I expect you to bring it to my attention. If something I do strikes you as odd, I would hope that you would find some way of communicating that to me."

"The only thing that strikes me as odd," said one of the aides, "is that you want our advice."

CHAPTER TWENTY-SIX

The next day, Tara spent some time in the archives of the Institution, searching out her mother's file. She was confronted by a number of questions. The file indicated that a Dr. Bauer had pronounced her mother deceased, and that Grace Maybury had been the nurse on duty. She noted that Maybury had written that her mother had suffered a series of seizures lasting from ten to fifteen minutes. Tara knew that there had been a standing order for Dilantin to be administered by injection for prolonged seizures. However her mother's record did not indicate that such an injection had been given.

"And why," Tara wondered, "if the seizures lasted for such a long time, was the doctor not summoned until after her mother had died?"

The record noted that although the death was unexpected, no autopsy was requested because the cause of death was verified by three attending staff members -- Grace Maybury, Doris Pitts, and Randolph Sinclair.

Tara also researched Ellie's record, taking special interest of a notation about her "hallucination" of a woman in a bathtub of blood and her claims that patients were being chained in the dungeon in the cellar. As much as the vivid description, Tara was taken by the date that the hallucination first appeared -- the same week as her mother's death.

According to the diagnosis sheet, Ellie was mentally retarded. However, Tara knew that hallucinations and delusions weren't consistent with such a diagnosis. Something was very wrong.

When she left the archives, Tara saw a familiar figure in the hallway. Instinctively, she crouched back. Although she recognized Grace Maybury immediately, she could only hope that the ten years since she'd last seen her would make her seem a stranger.

Director of Nursing now, Grace had aged a great deal in the past decade. Her struggles with Faith Byrd had taken a heavy toll. Even as she walked through the halls, Grace's time was almost up. Faith Byrd was working her evil magic.

CHAPTER TWENTY-SEVEN

Taking the next step in her climb to the top, Faith Byrd approached Doris Pitts.

"Pitts, I'd like a word with you," Faith said, an icy sharpness to her tone.

"Yes, Ms. Byrd?" Doris said.

"Have a seat, Pitts."

"No, thank you. I think I'll stand," Doris said, sensing danger.

Faith shrugged. "You know, for the past ten years you've been assigned to these self-care patients. For some reason, you have not been required to rotate to the less-desirable wards like all the other staff. This ludicrous favoritism has got to end."

"Favoritism?"

"That's right, Pitts. The time has come for a change in your situation."

"I...I don't know what you're talking about," Doris said, stammering.

"You don't? Well, let me make it plain for you then. I'm rotating you to A-10."

"A-10?"

"That's right. Dr. Ramsey has gone to a lot of trouble to institute his program on this unit. I intend to help make it a success," she said, her square jaw set, and her cold eyes staring into Doris Pitts's.

"I...I'll help make it a success," Pitts said, chilled to the bone now.

"Really?" Faith said, taunting her. "I hardly think so -- not based on your record. No, too much money is at stake and I don't think we can afford to have you on this unit now.

"You understand my position, don't you? I can't afford to have this program crippled by one uncooperative employee, the way you have always crippled the operation of this unit.

"No, your leaving will solve a number of problems, including the dissension that has been generated by you flaunting your preferred treatment, and by your lack of cooperation."

Faith smiled at Doris, knowing by the look in Doris's eyes that she was being very successful in rattling that skeleton in the closet. "Yes," she thought to herself, "this should set off some sparks. Maybe we'll have a great display of fireworks at Dunton."

However, striking the blow was not yet destroying Doris, and Faith was somewhat surprised when Doris suddenly asserted herself.

"I have no intention of going to work on that shit ward," she stated, controlling her voice. "I'll be staying right here, lady, and there's nothing you can do about it."

Faith's smile froze on her lips. "That's what you think, Pitts," she said, her voice filled with venom. "Be assured, you will be transferring to A-10."

Doris narrowed her eyes, then wheeled about and stormed from Faith Byrd's presence.

CHAPTER TWENTY-EIGHT

Doris Pitts went directly to Randy Sinclair's office. When she burst in, her heart was still pounding and she could no longer control the shakiness in her voice.

"That witch wants me moved to A-l0," she stated, pushing her face up close to him. "What are you going to do about it?"

Randy backed away, a little intimidated by her assertiveness.

"What the hell does she want to move you now for? It never mattered to her before?"

Doris leaned back and took a deep breath. "I think it has something to do with Laurie Canaday leaving," she said, making the connection for the first time. Then she shrugged.

"Who knows why a woman like that does anything?" Then she shivered. "How could I ever go over there to work? They'd just love to put the screws to me."

Randy looked at her, helpless. "But what the hell can I do about it? Things aren't the way they used to be. You know that as well as I do."

Doris came close again. "Look, I have two more years to put in on this Hill, and I have no intention of spending them on a shit ward! You got that? So if you don't want the whistle blown on you, then you'll manage to come up with something."

"Jesus," Randy sighed when Doris had left his office. He was in a quandary over what to do. Finally, he decided he would go and speak directly with Faith, even though he knew it would be a futile effort.

Worse than useless, the visit served to make Faith more suspicious than ever of Randy's relationship with Doris Pitts.

"May I ask why you've suddenly decided to transfer Doris Pitts now after having supported her during Laurie Canaday's efforts to have her removed from the unit?" Randy asked as he stood timidly in the doorway of Faith's office.

"That's none of your business," Faith answered simply. Then she fixed her eyes on Randy. "I don't know what's going on between the two of you, but what I do know is that the distribution of the staff is the concern of the administrator, not the staff psychologist."

Randy, though wounded by Faith's tone, did try. "It would be a shame to move her after all these years," he said. "I can't say I approve."

"Your approval is irrelevant," Faith said sharply. "Besides, I couldn't say I much approve of you or your permissive attitude, or your mouth.

"It might be of some interest to you that there's a new psychologist -- a woman -- who's just been hired in the Main Building. I understand that she'd love to come over here to the Annex to work with us." Faith paused for the most dramatic and cruel effect. "I've been considering asking her to do just that -- and telling them that they can have you back."

With that, Faith looked down at the paperwork on her desk, making it clear that she had nothing more to say. Randy began to offer a challenge, but decided against it. He turned meekly and slunk away.

As he walked down the hallway, back to his office, he felt a tightness in his throat, gripping him tighter and tighter, until he felt it as a real pain, and not just tightness.

"My God," he sighed, gasping for breath as he sat in one of the chairs lining the hallway.

He leaned his head back against the cold wall. He reached his hand up and felt the sweat drenching his hair. His face was cold and clammy to his touch. Suddenly, he was filled with the most frightening thoughts. He kept seeing Faith's vicious eyes piercing his own, reading his weaknesses, cutting him, deeper, deeper.

Randy tried to call out for help, but he couldn't find the strength to make any sound.

"What's happening to me?" he wondered.

For the first time in his life, Randy felt genuine fear -- the fear of impending doom -- of death. "I can't be having a heart attack," he told himself. "I'm too young. I've always taken care of myself. I'm healthy."

His mind quickly rifled through all the possibilities. He recalled that his father suffered from angina, and although it was sometimes frightening, he lived twenty-five years after his first heart attack.

At that moment, twenty-five years seemed like an eternity to Randy. "I'll have to see my doctor," he told himself. "I'll probably be given nitroglycerin tablets like my father was. Nothing to worry about."

Slowly, very slowly, the tightness in his throat subsided. By the time he felt well enough to get up, his clothes were soaked through. He took a deep breath, relieved to be feeling somewhat himself again.

He returned to his office to finish up some paperwork before going home. While there, he suffered a second and fatal heart attack.

He was discovered by a member of the janitorial crew.

The following day, the staff was notified that Randy had died.

CHAPTER TWENTY- NINE

No one took Randy's death more painfully than Doris Pitts. She had lost an influential supporter, and now was left with only one person to turn to -- Grace Maybury.

"She'd better make good of her promise to me," Doris said to herself, letting her thoughts drift back to a time ten years earlier, when she had been assigned to the female infirmary ward in the Main Building, under ward charge Grace Maybury.......

At the time, Grace was being considered for Director of Nursing, a position that she desperately wanted. Grace performed her tasks with an eye toward the Directorship, particularly the one of applepolishing Dr. Atherton.

Assigned to Grace's ward was patient Virgie Doyle. In addition to being confined to a wheelchair due to her crippling automobile accident, she was subject to epileptic seizures, often suffering a series of violent seizures known as status epilepticus. During these episodes, Virgie was in imminent danger of death.

In addition to her physical problems, Virgie was what was known as a 'problem patient'. Having been institutionalized for many years, she was well-versed in the Institution's rules and procedures. She carried tales from one shift to the other, and knew how to play the staff members against each other. She monitored the staff carefully for any infraction of the rules. She eavesdropped to get incriminating information, using the information to bargain for the modest 'special' privileges available at Dunton -- being allowed to say up late or to sleep in, or being given extra treats such as candy, drugs, or cigarettes.

Staff sometimes found themselves in the clutches of patients such as Virgie.

Which was exactly the position that Grace Maybury and Randy Sinclair found themselves in with Virgie. Tenaciously snooping, Virgie had discovered that Randy had begun an intimate relationship with sixteen-year old patient Ellie Matheson, a pretty, petite girl whose parents had 'hidden her away' because she was somewhat retarded.

When she noticed him paying particular attention to Ellie, Virgie began keeping careful notes on Randy. She wrote down how often, and for how long, he visited with the girl.

On one occasion, having become convinced of what was going on, she "accidentally" opened Ellie's door during one of Randy's visits.

Although Randy quickly pulled up the sheet, it was clear that both he and the young girl were naked in bed.

"Close the door, you old fool!" he shouted at Virgie.

Virgie held the door open a moment longer as a smile spread across her face. Then she slowly closed it, knowing that she could just as easily shut the door on his career.

If she had made his behavior public, he would have been dismissed immediately. More to the point, due to Ellie's age, he could easily have been sent to prison.

"Just what was the meaning of that?" Randy demanded, approaching Virgie after he had composed himself and left Ellie's room.

Virgie chuckled softly.

"Look, no one will believe anything you say." he challenged.

She looked at him and arched her eyebrows as if to say, "No? Who's deluded now?"

He knew she was right. He could feel his hands tremble and a curious tightening sensation come to his throat. He considered briefly making a deal with Virgie, something to buy her silence. But he knew that what Virgie had seen was so incriminating that she would never settle for cigarettes or treats. No, from that point on, she would own him.

Of course, Virgie was not the only one who knew of Randy's relationship with Ellie. Grace Maybury was aware of it and she voiced her strong disapproval to him many times.

"Forget that you could be fired, or go to jail," she said to him once. "It's wrong, just plain wrong."

His eyes flashed in anger when she said that.

"Wrong?" Who are you to tell me what's wrong?"

Grace's eyes widened but she remained silent.

"You know what I mean, don't you, Grace?"

"I...I..."

"No?" he asked, suddenly feeling that he had the upper hand.

"Perhaps I could help you. Let's see. According to my observations, there has been some hanky-panky going on in the medicine closet, particularly in the narcotic box."

"That's enough," she said firmly, looking away from him. It was clear to her that she had not kept hidden her illicit drug activity from his curious eyes.

"Stalemate?" he said, smiling.

Grace tightened her lips, frustrated and angry but ultimately stymied in her criticism.

"Stalemate," she said finally.

"Good," he said.

For many years, mutual blackmail had kept Grace's and Randy's secrets safe from discovery....except by Virgie Doyle.

CHAPTER-THIRTY

One afternoon, Virgie Doyle had silently wheeled herself to the chart room and watched as Grace Maybury opened the narcotic box with her special key and then exchanged the Darvon capsules with some of her own, which she had filled with sugar. Virgie watched as Grace poured the new pills into her purse.

The deed done, Grace turned to leave the chart room only to discover Virgie in the doorway.

"How long have you been there?" she demanded, taken by surprise.

Virgie smiled wickedly.

"I asked you a question!"

Virgie began to laugh -- a cruel cackle.

She didn't really have to answer. It was clear that she had been there "too long" from Grace's point of view -- and for her own good.

Although Virgie was silent then, she did speak -- many times -- later. Hardly a day went by without Virgie sidling her wheelchair

up close to Grace and whispering some comment about what she'd seen her do.

When Grace was offered the position of Director of Nursing, Virgie threatened to reveal what she knew about her if she left the ward. She did not want to lose the special privileges she was receiving from Grace in exchange for her silence.

Grace knew that if she accepted that position, she'd be putting herself in an extremely vulnerable position. What Virgie knew about her was hardly "little". If she were to reveal what she knew, it would ruin Grace's chances for the position she so desperately wanted, and would probably cost her her nursing career in the bargain. Grace saw Virgie as an obstacle to the position which she had coveted for so long.

It was 'complete bath day' and Grace was on duty. As she disrobed Virgie and eased her down into the tepid water, she was subjected to a continual diatribe of what would happen to her if she ever left the ward -- what would happen to her if Virgie ever told anyone what she'd seen her do that day in the chart room.

"I'll tell, I will, " Virgie said. "I'll tell everyone."

Grace dropped to her knees at the side of the tub and began to sponge the warm water over Virgie's shriveled body, trying to close her ears to Virgie's threats.

Suddenly, Virgie cried out, "The light! The light!"

Grace stiffened. She knew that a seizure was imminent. Virgie always saw a flash of light just before going into a seizure.

Grace relaxed, knowing what was going to happen next. She rested back on her haunches as Virgie's body became rigid. She watched with remarkable passivity as Virgie's jaw locked and her hands clenched at her sides. Her eyes were no longer focused on Grace, as her legs extended in the water, pulling her head down and under.

Grace rocked back and then stood up, never taking her gaze from Virgie. Virgie's violent convulsing splashed the water up over the side of the tub, sending it under Grace's feet.

Grace watched impassively as the convulsing stopped. As Virgie's muscles relaxed, she drew water deep into her lungs. Her eyes, which had been open and fixed at the beginning of her convulsion, never closed.

"Oh my God!" aide Doris Pitts screamed. Doris had come into the tub room to get a 'bath bundle' and had been shocked to see Virgie under the water and Maybury standing there, watching her impassively.

The sight of Virgie was most disturbing. Her eyes, still wide open, were more difficult to see as the water grew murky with the blood from her chewed tongue and the contents of her bladder and bowels, which had evacuated during her seizure.

Doris rushed past Grace and pulled Virgie's head above the water. Meanwhile, at the sound of Doris's scream, Randy had begun to run down the hall from Ellie Matheson's room, adjusting his clothing as he ran.

"It was an accident...an accident!" Grace was crying out. She started to convulse...I couldn't keep her head above the water."

"Then why didn't you call for help?" Pitts demanded accusingly. She had been aware of the relationship between Grace and Virgie, and although she didn't known the ultimate source, was fully aware of how much Grace hated her. Just then, Randy burst into the tub room.

"What the...?"

"She wanted her dead!" Doris said, staring up at Grace with Virgie's head in her hands and the front of her uniform stained with the murky water. "She killed her!"

Randy looked from Pitts to Maybury and back. "Okay, okay," he said, patting the air with his hands. "Let's just keep our heads here. I don't think this is the time..."

"You murdered her!" Doris said, narrowing her eyes at Grace.

"That's enough!" Randy said, trying to exert control over the situation. "Okay, let me think."

There was a short silence as Randy considered the options before him. "Now," he said, when he was ready to speak again, "let's look at this rationally."

"That's right," Grace said, picking up on his meaning. "There's no reason to get excited. I'm sure the world won't have any problem surviving her death."

Randy glanced at Virgie in the water and was secretly glad that his own secret had gone with her.

"Both of you help me clean up this mess and get her body back in bed before someone comes and sees us," Grace ordered.

"Before someone sees us?" Doris Pitts said. "What the...?"

Grace Maybury cut her off. "Keep your mouth shut and when I get to be the Director of Nurses, I'll take good care of you -- very good care of you. Do you understand? You'll never have to dirty your hands again."

Doris looked from Maybury to Virgie and back. She had worked for eight years on the very difficult wards, cleaning up after patients. The thought of never having to work like that again was quite appealing.

However, Doris didn't answer directly. Instead, she simply allowed Maybury and Randy to remove the body from the tub. They placed it in the wheelchair and then wiped it dry before dressing it in a johnny.

They wheeled it back to the room while Doris emptied the water from the tub and cleaned up the mess.

With everything cleaned up, Grace Maybury summoned the doctor on duty to the ward to pronounce Virgie dead. Dr. Bauer arrived at Virgie's room about ten minutes later.

"She died during a severe epileptic seizure," Grace explained when he got there.

"Hmm," Dr. Bauer said, taking down the sheet and looking at Virgie briefly. "Not surprising, given her history,"

"Yes," Randy agreed.

Dr. Bauer made the appropriate notations on the Doctor's Order Sheet without asking any further questions. After all, verification by two staff members in the death of a patient with a long prior history didn't usually demand lengthy questioning. But the true cause of her death would forever remain unrevealed -- or so it would seem at the time.

"I'll contact the family," the doctor said. Grace and Doris completed the postmortem care and quickly had Virgie's body removed to the Institution's morgue located at the Annex.

A short time later, Tara Doyle, Virgie's only child, arrived on her mother's ward where she was greeted by Dr. Bauer and Grace Maybury.

"We're terribly sorry," Dr. Bauer began, planning on launching into his set condolence speech. Generally, the family was less than upset when a family member in Dunton passed away. Often it was more of a burden removed, than a terrible event.

But Tara cut him off. Having noticed her mother's already stripped bed and her belongings removed, she asked, "Could I see my mother, please?"

"I think it would be better if you would wait until after the undertaker has prepared her," Grace Maybury said.

"I'd like to see my mother," Tara insisted. At fifteen, she was in her first year of high school and was considering a career in law. However, she had always been torn in that goal -- wanting to work in an environment where she could help people like her mother too.

However, her interest in law had made her assertive -- an attribute that she was exhibiting at Dunton that afternoon.

"I'd like to see my mother," Tara insisted.

Grace Maybury escorted Tara to the morgue.

After pulling out the receptacle containing Virgie's body, Grace stood back while Tara kissed her mother. She stroked her hair, then turned to Grace.

"Why is her hair wet?" she asked.

The color drained from Grace's face. "I..uh..when she died, she..banged her head. When we cleaned her up, we wet her hair..."

Tara nodded, seeming to accept the explanation. Meanwhile, Grace wondered how to slow the pounding of her heart.

CHAPTER THIRTY-ONE

Remembering the day that she had burst in on Virgie Doyle's death scene, Doris nodded to herself. "Yes, Grace had just better live up to her word. I'm awfully tired of keeping her dirty secret."

With that thought in mind, she hurried toward Grace's office, not bothering to knock as she burst in. "Maybury, I've only got two more years to put in on this Hill, and I don't intend to put them in working on a shit ward!"

Grace looked up, startled both by the entrance and by what Doris was saying. "What...?"

"Those bitches on A-10 are just waiting for me to come over so they can take out their revenge on me." She came closer to Grace's desk. "Look, I don't know why Faith is doing this to me now, but you've got to stop her. Right now."

"But..but..I don't have any authority over Faith," Maybury said softly. "She'd rather see me dead than do me a favor...I'm powerless in this, Doris. There's nothing I can do. It's useless to even try..."

Doris looked at Grace with a look of total disgust. Then she leaned even closer, narrowing her eyes. "Well, I'm sure you'll think of something -- something good. Because if you don't, I swear that you can kiss your goddamned career and your goddamned life away.

"I'm not going back to the bed wards, you understand? I'm never going back, and that's why you're going to keep the promise you made to me ten years ago. You remember, don't you, Maybury?"

"I.. I'll.. I'll try to do something, Doris. I'll try. You know how things have changed here..." her voice was pleading now and Doris Pitts was not in the mood to be understanding.

"I don't care what's changed and what hasn't. All I know is that I'm not going back, not now, not ever to a shit ward, and you're the one who's gonna make sure that I don't have to. Period."

Grace looked at Doris and felt the helplessness of having nowhere to turn. How could she possibly save Doris's position? Yet, how could she afford not to?

In her desperation, she decided she would go directly to Zeb Ramsey and possibly arrange a transfer for Doris to one of the easier wards in the Main Building.

"I'll try.. I'll do my best," she told her.

"You'd better do better than just try," Doris said in a most threatening tone.

After Doris left her office, Grace struggled to regain her composure. Once she did, she walked over to Zeb Ramsey's office and knocked lightly on his door.

"Come in," Zeb said.

"Dr. Ramsey..."

"Hello, Mrs. Maybury, come on in," he said, gesturing for her to take a seat.

Grace smiled humbly and sat down. She looked down at her hands while Zeb finished up some paperwork on his desk.

He looked up at Grace. "What can I do for you, Mrs. Maybury?"

"I... it's about Doris Pitts..."

Zeb's expression changed, hardened.

"Apparently Faith is planning on transferring her to A-10. I was wondering if you could find a place for her here in the Main Building..."

What Grace didn't know was that Faith had already taken care of the inevitability of her very request.

Zeb cleared his throat. "From what I understand, " he began, "Doris Pitts has been insubordinate, refusing to obey orders by her superiors. According to Faith, she's been the source of many of the problems at the Annex, and as you know, I've always taken a strong stand against transferring problems from one building to another."

Grace rubbed her forehead, trying to focus her thoughts. "But Faith wants to transfer Pitts to a bed ward! Isn't that transferring problems also?"

Zeb took a deep breath. "That's more like rotating staff," he said simply.

"But Pitts hasn't done that type of work in years?" Maybury said, not bothering to try to mask the desperate tone in her voice. She had to change Zeb's mind. However, her argument fell on deaf ears.

"Well then, isn't that all the more reason to transfer her? All staff should rotate, Mrs. Maybury. The fact that Doris Pitts hasn't in all these years is simply wrong. I'm sorry, but I simply can't overrule Faith's decision. I'm sure you agree."

However, Grace wasn't thinking of agreeing or of not agreeing. She was thinking that she was witnessing the end of her job and the life she'd built for herself.

Back in the privacy of her own office, she laid her head down on her desk. "That's it, that's the end of me," she thought sadly. "And that's final."

CHAPTER THIRTY-TWO

Doris Pitts's prediction that she wasn't going to be shown any mercy on A-l0 proved to be right on the money. From the moment she arrived, she was bombarded with offensive remarks about "slumming it" and was assigned the most difficult patients on the ward. The other staff watched her with amusement By quitting time, she was frustrated, angry and exhausted.

With what remaining energy she possessed, she made her way to Maybury's office. "You had better do something pretty quick!" she said. "If you have any aces to play, you'd better play them now, because I've had it!

"Do you hear me? I'm not working another day on that shit ward! You'd better listen good, Maybury, because I'm serious, dead serious. If I go -- and I swear this on a stack of Bibles -- if I'm going, I'm taking you with me."

Maybury lowered her eyes. "I understand," she said softly. Then she sighed. "Well, it was nice knowing you, Pitts."

Doris stared at Grace as she got up from her desk. "What the....?"

"Let's just say good-bye right now," Grace said, extending her hand to Doris. "I hate to say this, Pitts, but I have no options and no aces in the hole. I'm against the wall and I don't have any place to turn."

"What are you saying?" Doris demanded.

"What I'm saying," Grace continued wearily, "is that Faith has beaten me. I can't fight her because I have no weapons to fight with. Don't you see? She doesn't care about you. She's after me."

It wasn't long before Dunton's efficient grapevine began circulating rumors that Grace Maybury was contemplating leaving. When this patiently-awaited news reached Faith's ears, she knew that Grace's defeat was at hand. She went immediately to Zeb Ramsey's office, closing the door behind her when she entered.

"Hello, Faith," he said, unaware that this would not be just another one of her usual visits.

She smiled. "I've heard that Grace Maybury is considering resigning..."

Zeb made a face. "Ah, she was recently in my office on behalf of Doris Pitts, pleading with me to rescue her from reassignment to hard bed-ward duty. I thought it quite strange that a director of nurses would trouble herself so, for an aide -- especially one who's been so troublesome."

He looked directly at Faith. "Why now the decision to transfer Doris Pitts?"

"I've explained to you my reasons," Faith said coldly. "I shouldn't have to explain them to you again."

"No..no," Zeb said, "I was just..."

Faith cut him off. "I want to state my desire to hold Grace Maybury's position after she vacates it."

"Can't we at least wait for her to make that decision and inform me?" Zeb began, not wanting a confrontation at this time.

"No. I want your assurance that when she quits, I will be appointed to take her place."

"Faith, please, be realistic. I appreciate your interest and your desire, but it's really out of the question. Your background is simply inadequate to qualify you, and I don't know if I could survive the criticism I'd receive if I gave you such a promotion, when there are many nurses here who are far more qualified. No, I don't see how it can be done," he concluded, shaking his head and tugging at his beard.

"There may be others more qualified," Faith conceded icily, "but none of them have that something that I have."

Zeb looked at her, not sure what she meant.

"None of them have that special knowledge that I possess," she said lightly.

"Special knowledge?" he asked, still confused by what she was saying.

She laughed. "Yes, that special knowledge about a certain highly-placed administrator in this Institution who..." she paused, "now, how shall I phrase this? -- who witnessed an unfortunate "accident" involving an unfortunate patient who fell down and broke her leg. Do you recall such an incident?" she asked, narrowing her eyes as her voice turned cold.

His mouth dropped open but he didn't say anything.

"Get my meaning, Zeb?"

It became clear to him what she was doing. He nodded, defeated. "Yes, I get your meaning, Faith. I get it perfectly."

"Good." she said, leaning back and smiling with deep, self-satisfaction. "I'm glad to see you haven't lost your ability to think. After all, there's no reason to jeopardize that highly-placed administrator's position, is there?"

"No," Zeb said sadly as he shook his head.

"And we certainly wouldn't want to jeopardize his Annex grant, would we now?"

Zeb didn't bother replying. He was already thinking ahead to how he was going to appoint Faith to Grace's position and avoid the criticism that was sure to follow. "I suppose we could pad your record with some extensive private-duty experience," he said, his voice emotionless. "I imagine that would be the most difficult to disprove."

"I like that," she noted with approval. "Now, there's just one more thing," she said.

"What's that?" he asked, suddenly very weary.

"I'd like to get away from that 'nursing' image. It's so...feminine. Instead of 'Director of Nurses', why don't we change the title to 'Assistant Superintendent'?"

CHAPTER THIRTY-THREE

Zeb Ramsey was feeling a great deal of pressure. Among other things, there were Tara Doyle's constant complaints about Aaron Broderick's ill treatment of patients, which Zeb was helpless to act upon.

He needed to get Tara off his back, and he concluded that he'd be better off with her over at the Annex.

"But my work is in the Main Building," she countered.

"I know," Zeb said, "but Randy Sinclair's unfortunate passing has left me with a serious need in the Annex. I'd like you to take his position."

Tara realized that she had no alternative but to accept the transfer. Consequently, she did it as gracefully as she could. She knew that it would be more difficult to accomplish her mission from the Annex. Worse, she was concerned for her patients. After establishing a relationship with them, she was worried that they might feel she had deserted them. She was especially concerned for Ellie, but took solace in knowing that with Randy Sinclair's death, Ellie was freed from that particular hell.

In the Annex, Tara had to deal directly with Faith Byrd. That was the negative. On the positive side, she met Mathilda Hoxie, the lady with a "nose for news." Mathilda had been with the Institution for many years, and there wasn't much that happened that Mathilda didn't find out about. She gloried in tossing monkey wrenches into the works -- and always came out smelling like a rose.

Two of the people whom Mathilda currently enjoyed talking about were Faith and Rene. "They say there's somethin' funny goin' on between those two. They seem awful close for two women. When they arrived, they said they were goin' places, and they sure have.

"And I don't believe Della Frazier's injury was any accident. I believe her when she says a man threw her down and another hairy-faced man told him and a girl to just put her to bed and let her suffer. I know that Aaron Broderick ain't fit to take care of these patients, and I think his ass ought to be kicked down off of this Hill."

Tara listened to Mathilda without saying anything. There were a great many things going on and it was going to take some time to sort them out. However, one thing she was sure of, Faith was at the center.

"If I cozy up to her," Tara told herself, "and create some conflict between her and Rene, something might surface."

During her next conversation with Faith, Tara casually mentioned that she was looking for new living quarters. Hearing this, Faith's ears perked up.

"Really? I have a housemate right now, but she's been talking about moving. If she does, I'll be sure and let you know."

"That would be great," Tara said, coloring her show of enthusiasm with just a hint of seductiveness.

Then she brought up Rene. "She really doesn't have the background for the position of 'facilitator', and that is causing dissension among the staff who already feel resentment for her because of the special position Rick created for her. It would be far more appropriate for me to assume that position.

After Tara left, Faith considered what the new psychologist had been saying. In her mind, she reviewed with sadistic delight her two-fold strategy for placing Rene on Zeb's Behavior Modification unit. Rene's training had qualified her for the 'facilitator' position which appropriately replaced Laurie Canaday's position, and her witnessing of Zeb's cover-up of the Della Frazier incident helped put him where Faith wanted him.

Faith had known that there were real problems on Zeb's unit. There had been numerous complaints of patient abuse, mostly involving attendant Aaron Broderick -- complaints that were threatening Zeb's position and funding for his program. The program had, in fact, been put on notice. Zeb had threatened to fire Aaron, so Aaron was more than willing to conspire with Faith and Rene in a scheme to set him up.

Faith's plan was for Aaron to assault a patient when Zeb would enter the unit and be a witness to it. Faith knew that Zeb would opt just to cover it up to save his position, and when he did, he would be at her mercy.

Aaron delightfully chose Della Frazier as his subject. He didn't like Della, and Della didn't like him because he'd been rough with her a few times for defying him. So it was not difficult to provoke her into the incident which resulted in grave injury to her.

True to Faith's prediction, Zeb warned them to say nothing, lest their jobs be jeopardized. Then he was where she wanted him.

The pleasure that this line of reasoning brought to Faith blurred into her recollection of her conversation with Tara. She hadn't missed the seductive clues that Tara had given. No, she had taken full note of them.

"I wonder if she understands what it means to be really loved," Faith thought to herself as she considered the young woman's sexual preference. As she did, she found herself longing to find out, to be with the new young and attractive woman.

The more she thought about Tara, the more she despised Rene. "That bitch has worn out her welcome," she told herself, convincingly. Indeed, the more Faith thought about it, the more she realized that Rene's position and knowledge made her as much a threat as an ally. "She's getting too smart, too demanding," she complained to herself. "I wish to hell she'd just drop dead."

She considered the suggestion of Tara's to demote Rene back to an aide. "That's not such a bad idea," she told herself. "Not a bad idea at all."

CHAPTER THIRTY- FOUR

Tara Doyle was not at the Annex long when the three people listed on her mother's record as having attended her death were no longer at the Institution. Randy had died of a heart attack. Then, in a curious sequence of events that had many tongues wagging, Grace Maybury and then Doris Pitts retired. Doris's and Grace's retirements were the most disturbing. Each had only two years to go before receiving full retirement benefits.

"What could have prompted them to leave so early and so suddenly?" was the question on everyone's lips.

Faith Byrd's appointment to Grace's position created a great deal of dissension. Petitions circulated throughout the Institution protesting her appointment. Grievances were filed by those who were better candidates -- all ignored by Zeb Ramsey.

The staff was delighted as Rene Boutelle was demoted back to an aide, and Tara Doyle assumed the role of 'facilitator'

"She should have been fired," Margaret Putnam said to Tara, of Rene, "instead of just being demoted." Tara was assisting the new team leader of Doris Pitts's old ward with her patient treatment plans.

"I used to work evenings on this ward, and I overheard her and Randy Sinclair and Doris Pitts scaring Minnie, Dora, and Pearl out of being discharged so they could keep them here working on this ward. Can you imagine?"

Tara only shook her head sadly. "I'm afraid I can," she said.

"If only Doris would have been transferred when Laurie Canaday was Unit Chief, she could have done her job, and maybe she wouldn't have left..."

"She left because of Doris Pitts?" Tara asked.

"Yes, and all those who wouldn't let her do her job."

Margaret shared many things with Tara about the circumstances which led up to the resignation of Laurie Canaday, giving Tara much food for thought.

Rene was livid. She wasn't blind. She saw the glances exchanged between Faith and Tara. She could mark her own decline with Tara's arrival.

As much as she despised Tara, her real anger was directed toward Faith. "I helped her get to where she is," she reminded herself. "I stuck my neck way out for that two-timin' bitch."

Now, all she thought about was a way to bring Faith down without destroying herself in the process.

CHAPTER THIRTY- FIVE

Meanwhile, Ellie Matheson began to wonder where 'doctor' Sinclair was. Never before had so much time elapsed between his visits. Some days she remained in her room, convinced that he would come through the door any minute. However, the minutes and days continued without his appearance. She wondered if now she could tell people about the day she saw the bathtub of blood.

"And what about my treatments?" she thought. In spite of his many warnings and threats, she wondered who she could tell.

She liked the new lady 'doctor' who had come to her ward and spent time with her. "She is pretty," Ellie thought to herself. Her black hair reminded her of the silken hair that had been on a doll she once had.

"And she likes me," Ellie thought. "She said she'd be my sister. I always wanted a sister who loved me."

Tara decided that she would visit Ellie every now and then, even though she had been transferred to the Annex. When she told Ellie that Randy Sinclair was dead, Ellie screeched her delight. "Now I won't have any more treatments! Now I won't ever have to go down to the dungeon in the cellar to be chained!"

Although those words and that reaction were soon lost in Ellie's mind, they didn't vanish from Tara's consciousness. The words were almost verbatim what she'd read in Ellie's record down in the Institution's archives.

"Everything's so close," Tara told herself. "I can see all the loose ends dangling in front of me. But how will I bring them together?"

"'Doctor' Sinclair can never hurt you again," she told Ellie. "You can tell me about your 'treatments' now, and why you were afraid of being chained in a dungeon down cellar."

Ellie believed that she had found the person to tell her secrets to. Yet it was so hard.

"I...I can't," she stammered, wanting to relieve herself of her burdens but having such terrible trouble doing so. "I can't say it."

Tara leaned forward and put her hand on Ellie's "You must, Ellie," she said urgently. "I'm here to help you. You can try!"

That seemed to open a spigot for Ellie. All she had to do was try. And once she tried, succeeding came swiftly. In a maddening rush, she unleashed her horrible secrets -- the treatments she had been subjected to, and the events of that day so long before, surrounding the murder of Tara's own mother.

"I sneaked up to the tub room," Ellie related, "behind 'Doctor' Sinclair, after we heard a horrible scream. I peeked through the crack in the door and saw Virgie in a bathtub of blood. I saw Mrs. Pitts look at Mrs. Maybury and say, 'You murdered her'.

"When they put Virgie in the wheelchair," Ellie continued, "I knew they would come out soon, so I hurried back to my room. I peeked through the window in my door and saw them wheel Virgie into her room across the hall.

"Soon the big blond doctor came and went into the room. In a little while, they wheeled Virgie out on a stretcher -- all covered up. I never saw her again.

"Please don't tell Mrs. Maybury or Mrs. Pitts," Ellie begged when she had finished, her face flushed and her cheeks streaked with tears.

"I won't, Ellie," Tara promised, "and you must promise never to tell anyone else your secrets."

"I promise!" Ellie said.

Tara continued to talk to Ellie, calming her down, and easing her out of this remarkable session. All the while, she was exulting in her mind -- she had received her answer. Grace's and Doris's punishments were in her hands.

CHAPTER THIRTY-SIX

Zeb Ramsey sat at his desk, rubbing his forehead and tugging at his beard. He was weary of Faith Byrd, weary of the constant complaints he was receiving about her, weary of her manner, and weary of everything about her. But even the complaints about Faith paled next to the complaints he was receiving about Aaron Broderick's ill treatment of the patients. He was beginning to regret covering up Aaron's violent assault on patient Della Frazier.

"I did it to preserve my program and my career," he told himself. "Damn that patient for shooting her mouth off, and damn those who've made such an issue of it, putting me in this position."

As he was consoling himself in the fact that he had reassigned Tara Doyle to the Annex, and had at least gotten her off his back, he looked up to see her entering his office. She had come there directly after her visit with Ellie Matheson.

"I have just learned that patients on Aaron Broderick's ward are spending too much time in seclusion rooms," she said angrily, "courtesy of that fine attendant of yours. Well, it won't be long before we see just how caring your Aaron Broderick really is. Then we'll see how long he stays here."

Watching Zeb closely for his reaction, believing him to be the "hairy-faced man" referred to by Della, she said, "You see, it won't be long before Della Frazier will be able to verify in death what she cannot convince anyone of in life."

"What are you saying?" Zeb said, struggling to maintain control.

"I happen to know that Della does not have much longer to live," Tara told him. "The osteomyelitis which resulted from her injury has not responded to treatment, and her condition is deteriorating fast. Dr. Bauer has pre-arranged for her body to be autopsied, and he said that that will show conclusively whether or not her injury was deliberately inflicted. If it was, her death will be ruled a homicide.

"We'll see if there's not an indictment brought against your Aaron Broderick this time," she said as she stomped out of his office.

Zeb felt as though a noose were tightening around his neck.

"I may have more to lose now than my program and my career," he told himself.

Then his face hardened. In that moment, he began hatching a plan whereby Della's body would never reach the pathology room. "Aaron and Rene will assist me. They have as much and more at stake than I do," he told himself. "The truth will not come out!"

CHAPTER THIRTY-SEVEN

Grace Maybury sat up straight in bed, drenched in sweat and her heart pounding in her chest. Although the phone call had been three nights earlier, she had been plagued by nightmares as if she'd only just hung up the receiver.

"You gave me empty capsules for days, didn't you?" the voice demanded. "You wanted me to have convulsions and drown! You murdered me!"

Grace shook her head, her eyes wide with terror. "I must take something," she told herself, starting to get up. She was stopped by the ringing of the phone.

She froze. She didn't want to answer it but she couldn't make her hand stop reaching for the receiver.

"What do you want?" she asked, her voice trembling.

"This is Virgie," the voice said. "Help me! Lift my head up! I'm drowning!"

Then the calls started coming every midnight, with the voice giving one more detail of the crime -- making one more plea for mercy.

Grace was distraught. Having nowhere to turn without exposing herself, she became more and more agitated and unable to function.

"It must be Virgie's spirit," she told herself. "No one else could know these things."

One night while preparing for bed, she consumed three times her usual dosage of medication to dull her horror, and followed this with a hot bath to relax her. After falling into a deep stupor while in the tub, her head slumped into the water.

Doris Pitts read in the newspaper the next day that Grace Maybury had drowned in the bathtub. Blood studies indicated that she had an excessively high level of barbiturates in her system at the time, most likely producing drowsiness which resulted in her drowning. Doris couldn't help but be struck by the irony of Grace dying in a bathtub.

"Just like Virgie Doyle," she thought.

That afternoon, Doris's phone rang.

"Hello?" she said.

"This is Virgie," the voice said.

Doris's jaw dropped.

"I have drowned Grace Maybury in her bathtub. You're next."

Doris ran from her house, terrified and hysterical, screaming over and over, "She's come from the grave to kill me," as she rushed into the street.

She was ultimately transported to Dunton in a frenzy, after police were summoned to subdue her.

Doris was admitted to Dunton. Her condition was diagnosed as psychotic episode, characterized by morbid, paranoid delusions -- etiology unknown.

CHAPTER THIRTY- EIGHT

On the day that Della Frazier died, two figures waited impatiently in a vehicle in view of the entrance to the Institution's morgue at the Annex. Rene had notified Zeb of Della's death as planned, and of the expected arrival time of the undertaker, who was past due.

"I wish he would hurry and get here," Zeb said nervously, concerned that he and Aaron would be seen there together. "According to Rene's information, he should have been here a half hour ago."

Finally, a long, black vehicle backed up to the morgue entrance. The driver removed a gurney from the back and wheeled it into the building, as Zeb and Aaron anxiously watched and waited, hardly breathing.

A few moments later, he re-appeared with the gurney, bearing a shrouded human form, and returned it to the rear of the vehicle.

When the undertaker re-entered the building for the belongings and to sign receipts for them and the body, as was customary, Zeb shouted excitedly, "GO! NOW! I'll be right behind you."

Aaron sprang from Zeb's vehicle to board the hearse containing Della's remains.

They drove half-way down the hill before stopping side by side. Obscured by the winding roadway, they dashed to the rear of the vehicles and hurriedly threw each open. Adrenaline pouring into their blood, they snatched Della's body and transferred it from one vehicle to the other.

So absorbed were they in their haste to be on their way, they failed to notice the watchful eyes of Tara Doyle observing them from a safe distance.

*　　*　　*　　*　　*　　*　　*　　*　　*　　*　　*　　*

Since baiting Zeb with regard to an autopsy planned for Della, Tara had been keeping him under very close surveillance. His look of desperation at her mention of the word "homicide" had confirmed her suspicion of his involvement in the incident, and convinced her that he would go to any length to save his skin.

Following in her car behind him and Aaron, her surveillance had taken her along the deserted Willow Pond Road one afternoon, to a secluded dirt road.

A short distance onto the dirt road, they had stopped. Anxiously, Tara had left her car in order to follow more closely on foot.

Proceeding cautiously in the thick wooded area to keep out of sight, branches cutting into her face and legs, she had seen them -- seen them removing shovels from the rear of the car and disappearing into the woods.

Reeling from shock, she had turned and, with pounding heart, unsteadily retraced her steps.

*   *   *   *   *   *   *   *   *   *   *   *

Now, watching their ghoulish activity with Della's body, Tara was filled with satisfaction. "I'll give them some time to reach their destination," she told herself, "and then I'll put the police on their trail."

On the dirt road leading to the grave they had dug for Della, Zeb and Aaron, engrossed in the task at hand, did not notice the police cruiser following them, nor did they notice two policemen approaching as they were about to deposit Della's corpse in the grave.

Suddenly, the sound of a loud voice echoing through the woods shook them to their very roots.

"Police! Freeze!" ordered one policeman, his service revolver drawn as he advanced toward them with cautious steps. "Put your hands on top on your heads."

Zeb and Aaron stood dumbfounded as they were read their rights and handcuffed by the second policeman, who then led them back to the police cruiser and sent for an ambulance to pick up Della's body.

When Zeb regained control of his tongue, he asked the officers, "How did you know?"

"An eye witness notified police that she had seen you two murder this woman and stuff her body into the trunk of your car," related the first policeman.

"Unlucky for you, she was able to give us your exact location and license number," added the second.

Faith Byrd, sitting proudly behind the huge executive desk in the large, plush office occupied a short time earlier by Grace Maybury, had been dictating a memo to Grace's former secretary, when the call had come from the undertaker stating that his vehicle containing Della's remains had been stolen.

"It's been found, though," he had been quick to add, his voice quivering in disbelief, "half-way down the hill, but the body is gone!"

"My God," Faith had exclaimed, "someone has taken Della's body?"

"Yes," he had told her, "and this is the first time anything like this has ever happened to me. I've notified the police."

"Isn't that the patient they went to court about?" the secretary had asked.

"Yes," Faith had responded, disconcerted by that bizarre coincidence.

Faith's feelings of amazement at the report from the undertaker waned against those of profound shock at the subsequent report from the police.

"We want to let you know that the body missing from your institution was found in the possession of two white males trying to bury it," the caller stated.

His identification of Zeb and Aaron as those responsible, in answer to Faith's inquiry, set her body vibrating like a leaf in the breeze.

Returning the phone to its cradle, she barely heard the caller's last remark, "The body has been returned to its rightful place."

Faith dismissed the secretary and immediately sent for Rene.

Distraught at Faith's news of this unhappy turn of events, Rene stammered as she attempted to recount the plan to prevent Della's autopsy.

"What autopsy?" Faith snapped.

"The autopsy that would have sh...shown that D...Della had been deliberately thrown." Then, fighting back tears, fearing for what would become of her now, Rene continued, "Tara told Zeb that if that proved to be so, her death would be ruled a ho...homicide."

"I don't know where Tara Doyle got her information," Faith stated, "but if there had been any plan for an autopsy, I'd have been the first to know about it.

"And now," she scolded, "do you see what your antics are going to mean for you?" She answered her own question, "You'll be lucky if it's just your jobs."

Rene didn't answer, but quietly left, consoled only in the hope that perhaps now, Faith would get what was coming to her.

But Faith had no such concern. She felt secure -- secure in the fact that the only two people who could implicate her in this matter could not do so without incriminating themselves.

"I will be the next superintendent," she told herself, her heart pounding with excitement as she threw out her chest and lifted her head high.

At the police station, when the true facts of the matter were finally brought to light, and the body was identified as that reported missing by the undertaker, Zeb and Aaron were released from custody.

However, the implication of this incident sparked the interest of the district attorney, having failed in an earlier effort to get an indictment against this same man for his alleged assault on this very woman. Zeb and Aaron were advised not to leave Somerset, as a new hearing would be sought.

"See what your lack of control has done for us," Zeb yelled at Aaron, as they were leaving police headquarters. "I should have fired you long ago, before you had a chance to totally destroy me -- you and that goddam bitch, Tara Doyle."

Aaron remained silent, implying agreement with Zeb's perception of the incident.

"After all," he thought to himself, "lack of control would probably go easier for me than actually planning to thump the crazy old broad so we could blackmail him for coverin' it up."

CHAPTER THIRTY- NINE

Acting Superintendent Faith Byrd called all her available staff together to make some very important announcements.

"First," she began, in her typically overbearing manner, "I wish to announce the suspension of Superintendent Zeb Ramsey, along with attendant Aaron Broderick, for their inappropriate and totally bizarre act of confiscating the body of Della Frazier with the intention of burying it."

The silence in the room was deafening. Staff persons just looked at one another in horror, trying to cope with what they were hearing.

"And next," Faith continued, "I wish to announce my appointment as Dunton's acting superintendent."

Mumblings could be heard across the room by those whose rightful claims to advancement had been so blatantly disregarded in deference to her.

"I hope that son-of-a-bitch Aaron Broderick will finally get his ass kicked off this Hill," Mathilda Hoxie called out, "and that 'weirdo', Zeb Ramsey -- he don't belong here either, the way he let that Broderick treat them patients."

"Does this mean that Della was telling the truth?" asked one of the nurses -- "that her injury was no accident?"

"I don't know," responded Faith, "but their actions would certainly imply guilt."

"But why would they want to take her body and bury it?" asked one of the aides.

"There is going to be a hearing," Faith assured them, "which I am certain will provide the answer to that, and hopefully get them what they deserve."

Aide Margaret Putnam listened callously to Faith's announcement that yet another fancy-titled, do-nothing executive had bitten the dust.

"What difference does it make to us anyway?" she said to the A-2 aide, Faye Garland, who was sitting next to her. "It doesn't matter to us or the patients if the Zeb Ramseys or the Nathan Strenges, or the Hal Zachariases or the Faith Byrds, or this 'director' or that 'director'..."

"Or this 'resource' person, or that 'resource' person," echoed Faye, "are here or not. We don't ever see them."

"And I've barely even heard their names," continued Margaret.

"I wonder how much money they make for attending all those meetings and all those conferences," Faye said resentfully.

"I know one thing," replied Margaret, "they don't have any connection with how we aides on the wards care for our patients."

They were jolted from their verbal exchange as Faith continued, "I would like to announce some staffing changes that I intend to make."

The atmosphere in the room changed to one of uneasiness.

"I think," Faith continued -- "I think we can return you to the Annex, Mrs. Bagley. We can't seem to find a use for you over here in the Main Building. Mathilda Courtland can resume being your assistant as before."

"And you, Tara" -- speaking in her *sweet* voice, and flashing a broad smile -- "I know you've always preferred working in the Main Building, so I'm going to bring you back, and you can also assist me some."

With tongue in cheek, Tara expressed delight. They exchanged seductive glances while Rene looked on -- her face distorted by fury.

"That will be all for now," Faith announced brusquely. "You're all excused."

"I wonder if she'd smile at you so sweetly if she knew all that I know about you," Rene reminded Faith, hurrying to catch up with her as she strutted out of the conference room and down the corridor.

"Well, she won't find out anything from you, will she?" taunted Faith, "that is unless you'd like to go to jail."

"It would almost be worth going to jail," Rene countered, "to see you get what's coming to you, you witch."

Her square jaw set, and an evil cast to her eyes, Faith growled out her contempt for Rene, "I don't need you and I don't want you. I'm sick of your stupid antics, and I'm sick of you."

With that and a toss of her head, she turned from Rene and was on her way.

Left standing in the hallway, scorned and alone, Rene watched her former mate strutting pompously down the hallway -- the Institution's highest-ranking official -- a circumstance which never would have happened without her.

"And where did it all get me?" she asked herself, bitterly. "Where is the plum of a job that was supposed to have been mine? -- plucked from me in favor of Tara Doyle," she reminded herself, resentfully. "And what am I now? -- a lowly aide on a 'shit' ward."

"No," she told herself, convincingly, "the joys of freedom wouldn't be nearly so tasty as the sweetness of revenge."

CHAPTER FORTY

The trial of Aaron Broderick was attended by all available staff from Dunton Mental Institution, particularly those from the evening and night shifts whose working hours permitted it.

At an earlier hearing, the prosecuting attorney's request for an indictment had been granted, the presiding judge having considered the evidence sufficient to hold Aaron over for trial.

On advice of his attorney, Aaron pled not guilty to the charge of assault brought against him.

Acting Superintendent Byrd herself was in attendance at the trial, patiently waiting for her way to be cleared to Dunton's highest office.

"This should put an end to Zeb Ramsey," she told herself, confidentially. "Even if nothing can be proven against him, he'll never be allowed to return to Dunton -- not after all this bizarre publicity."

Tara was sitting with aide Margaret Putnam. Margaret's many confidences to Tara had greatly contributed to Tara's suspicions regarding Faith's strange rise to power.

The first person to take the stand was prosecution witness Sarah Archer, the eleven-to-seven-shift aide who first reported Della Frazier's injury.

"I noticed in the morning, about five-thirty, when I was about to give her A.M. care, that she was wide awake, not movin' a muscle, and that she was layin' exactly the same as when I checked her the night before, when I came on duty," Sarah testified.

"And what time was that?" asked the prosecutor.

"I checked her a little before eleven P.M. during rounds," Sarah responded.

"What did you do then?" asked the prosecutor.

"I asked her why she was awake and why she was layin' so stiff."

"What was her answer?" he asked.

"She told me that she was hurtin'."

"Go on," directed the prosecutor.

"I asked her where she was hurtin', and she put her hand on her left thigh. I pulled the covers down and saw that her left buttock and thigh were reddened and swollen. The skin was broken and I could see bone. She had been incontinent."

"Tell us what happened then," said the attorney.

"I asked her how that happened, and she told me that a man threw her over his shoulder to the floor and that another hairy-faced man told him and a woman to put her to bed and did nothin' for her pain."

"And what action did you take?" asked the prosecutor.

"First I called the duty doctor, who was Dr. Mezummi. I cleaned her up as best I could, and made out an Incident Report for Mrs. Maybury, the Director of Nurses."

After the prosecuting attorney thanked Sarah, the defense attorney said he had just one question for her.

"Have you ever known these patients under your care to make up stories, Miss Archer?"

"Yes," responded Sarah.

"Thank you," he said, "I have no more questions."

Dr. Mezummi was the second person to testify.

"Please tell us what you found when you were summoned to the ward by Miss Archer," the prosecutor asked.

"I found patient Della Frazier to be in acute distress, lying rigidly in bed. Further examination revealed a compound fracture of her left leg, obviously complicated by an infection."

"And what action did you take at that time?"

"After medicating her for pain, and applying a dressing and splint to her left leg, I made arrangements to send her to the Medical Center."

"Did you question the staff as to the cause of this injury?" asked the attorney.

"Yes," replied Dr. Mezummi.

"And what were you told?"

"Mr. Broderick mentioned that he vaguely remembered the patient tripping and falling over him and that he didn't think it significant at the time. Miss Boutelle corroborated that statement, although there was no documentation of such an incident on the patient's record."

"And what was the final outcome of Mrs. Frazier's injury, Doctor?" asked the prosecutor.

"She became bedfast," he answered, "and developed osteomyelitis which did not respond favorably to treatment."

When asked if it was his professional opinion that Della Frazier's osteomyelitis resulted from delayed treatment of her injury, he replied that it was.

The defense attorney had no questions for Dr. Mezummi.

Mathilda Hoxie was next to be called to the witness stand, and after being duly sworn, virtually repeated what Sarah Archer had to say, regarding Della's version of her injury.

When examined by the defense attorney, she was asked, "Have you ever known any of your patients to make up stories?"

"I don't think these patients would make up stories about somethin' like this," she replied.

"That's not what I asked you," he shot back. "Have you ever known any of your patients to make up stories?"

"Yes, I guess so," she replied, with reservation.

After the noon recess, it was Tara Doyle's turn to testify. Asked why she believed Della was telling the truth about her injury, she replied, "I have been aware for quite some time of Aaron Broderick's ill treatment of patients. I reprimanded him myself, regarding his abuse, and threatened to go to Zeb Ramsey, but he defiantly ignored me and my threats."

"Did you ever report him to Zeb Ramsey?" asked the prosecutor.

"Yes, I did," replied Tara," many times, to no avail."

"You mean he took no action whatsoever?" the prosecutor asked.

"I mean -- he totally disregarded my complaints, and firmly defended Aaron Broderick's actions as efforts to teach the patients responsibility. That's when I began to suspect that he was somehow implicated, and decided to bait him, as I mentioned at the hearing, in the hope of proving it."

"And as you also testified at the hearing, you followed him and Aaron to a makeshift grave, and then watched their attempt to hide the evidence of the assault on this woman which ultimately resulted in her death?"

The defense attorney objected to this statement, and the objection was sustained. He had no questions for Tara.

"Della didn't like me for some reason," Aaron testified, when asked by his attorney to relate the circumstances leading up to his alleged assault on her.

"She was always calling me nasty names, and when I thought she was going to hit me, I completely lost control and....I am very sorry for what happened," he whined, trying to feign remorse.

"Why did you not report the incident when you realized that the patient had been hurt?" asked his attorney.

"I didn't think she was hurt seriously," he said, "and besides, Zeb Ramsey happened to come onto the ward just at that time, and told me not to."

"And why do you suppose he told you not to report it?" the attorney asked.

"He said that we'd lose our jobs and funding for the program. It had been put on notice."

"And Zeb Ramsey is your boss, isn't he?" the attorney asked.

"Yes, he is," replied Aaron.

The prosecutor showed no mercy for Aaron's lack of self-restraint when it was his turn to ask the questions.

"Why do you suppose Della Frazier didn't like you and wanted to hit you? -- pushing her around a little, were you?" he asked sarcastically.

"Oh, no," replied Aaron, "I love those patients. It's just that I have a hard time controlling my temper sometimes."

"On the contrary, didn't you deliberately and maliciously assault that helpless old woman, causing her fatal injury?" the prosecutor challenged.

The defense attorney objected, the objection was sustained, and Aaron was allowed to step down.

When Zeb Ramsey was called as a hostile witness for the defense, he approached the stand with head and shoulders bent as though under the weight of a heavy burden -- the burden of worry for his career and his future. Evidence was stacking up strongly against him. Seemingly, his crime was the greater of the two, death being due primarily to delayed treatment, rather than the injury itself.

"Please give us your best recollection of the events, as they appeared to you, which led up to the injury of Della Frazier," directed Aaron's attorney.

"Just as I entered the ward," Zeb began, his voice trembling, "I saw the defendant grab her hand and hold it onto a mop handle, forcing her to mop the floor."

"Could Mr. Broderick have been assisting Mrs. Frazier in washing the floor?" asked the attorney.

"It didn't appear that way to me," replied Zeb.

"What did you see next?" the attorney asked.

"I saw him lift her part-way over his shoulder, and then throw her to the floor." Zeb said.

"Could it have been possible that Mr. Broderick was just protecting himself from being struck by this patient, and that in the skirmish, she slipped on the wet floor and fell?"

"That was not how it appeared to me," Zeb insisted.

"You are Mr. Broderick's boss, are you not?" Aaron's lawyer asked, threateningly.

"That is correct," Zeb replied.

"And you ordered him and Rene Boutelle to just put Mrs. Frazier to bed, and they did that. Is that correct?" he asked accusingly."

"That is correct," Zeb repeated.

"And it was your decision not to seek medical help after you realized that Mrs. Frazier had been injured. Is that not also correct?" asked the attorney.

"Yes," replied Zeb, "That is also correct."

"Thank you." said the attorney. "I have no more questions.

"What made you think that the defendant was forcing the deceased to mop the floor?" the prosecutor asked.

"He appeared very angry," replied Zeb, "and she appeared to be resisting him."

"Is it your practice to use the patients for ward work?" he asked contemptuously.

"That was her assigned task -- part of our program," Zeb responded defensively.

"And," taunted the prosecutor, "I take it she was not being too cooperative."

"That is correct," said Zeb.

"Getting back to Mrs. Frazier's injury, please tell us in detail what you saw happen after she turned to Mr. Broderick and raised her arm," directed the prosecutor.

"He lifted her part-way over his right shoulder, and then appeared to throw her down. Her left leg took the brunt of the fall," Zeb related, weariness creeping into his voice.

"Why did you not seek medical help for Mrs. Frazier's injury?" inquired the prosecutor.

"Because my program had been put on notice -- to save my program for the ultimate good of all the patients," Zeb exclaimed.

"Please tell us the circumstances of your program being put on notice," requested the prosecutor.

"Because -- because there are some people, especially nurses, who'd rather pamper patients and make them dependent," Zeb answered angrily, "who refuse to understand our techniques of teaching responsibility or realize the benefits that can be derived from my program."

"I have just one more question for you, Mr. Ramsey," the prosecutor said. "Did Aaron Broderick express any desire at all to obtain medical help for Della Frazier after she was injured?"

"No, he did not," replied Zeb.

Rene had been sitting alone during the trial, looking forward to her day in court. Now and again she would be the object of good-enough-for-you glances from aides who had resented her special treatment and condescending attitude.

When she rose to take her turn in the witness box, Faith smiled sweetly at her -- for the troops, of course -- but was suddenly gripped by fear, seeing Rene return her smile, equally sweet, and carry herself confidently to the front of the courtroom.

"During the original hearing of this case, you concurred with Aaron Broderick's testimony that the deceased patient tripped over him and fell, and that was how she sustained her injury," began the defense attorney, consulting the transcript of that hearing.

Rene, eager for revenge, and having prepared herself for when this time would come, answered his question very matter-of-factly. "No, that is not true."

The presiding judge looked over at her questioningly, and the attorney asked her to please explain.

Rene then proceeded to lay bare Faith's whole nasty plan for "getting to the top", holding everyone in the courtroom spellbound.

Pouring out her anger and indignation, she described in detail, being used by Faith, from the day of their arrival at Dunton, to scheme and plot the downfall of all in Faith's path to the top.

"Do you see Faith Byrd in the courtroom now?" asked the attorney, when she had finished her testimony.

"Yes," Rene answered. "She's leaving the courtroom right now."

"Don't allow that woman to leave!" ordered the judge.

The crowd, which had been listening in shocked silence, erupted into pandemonium as Faith Byrd, struggling to free her arm from the bailiff's hold, began screaming at Rene.

"Bitch!" she shouted, "you're going down with me, you miserable little wretch!"

"It will be well worth it! Rene shot back, before the judge had a chance to yell, "ORDER," in an attempt to re-establish control of the trial.

The crowd grew silent again and the judge called for a recess.

Tara struggled to control her delight. She had fulfilled her mission to avenge her mother's death and had succeeded in exposing the evil that had taken possession of the Institution.

"And now," she told herself with proud satisfaction, "justice is not far away."

"Tara! Tara!" exclaimed Margaret Putnam, who had been sitting next to her, "look at the woman in the red jacket, on the other side of the room. That's Laurie Canaday, and that's Sharon Lovejoy sitting next to her. Wouldn't it be great if they would come back to Dunton?"